Also in the

ROBOT RACES

series:

Rainforest Rampage

Arctic Adventure

Desert Disaster

First published in 2013 by Curious Fox,
an imprint of Capstone Global Library Limited,
7 Pilgrim Street, London, EC4V 6LB
Registered company number: 6695582

www.curious-fox.com

Text © Hothouse Fiction Ltd 2013

Series created by Hothouse Fiction
www.hothousefiction.com

The author's moral rights are hereby asserted.

Cover illustration by Spooky Pooka
Cover design by Mandy Norman

ISBN 978 1 78202 048 6

1 3 5 7 9 10 8 6 4 2

A CIP catalogue for this book is available from the British Library.

Typeset in Avenir by Hothouse Fiction Ltd

Printed and bound by CPI Group (UK) Ltd, Croydon, CRO 4YY

MIX
Paper from
responsible sources
FSC® C020471

With special thanks
to David Grant

CHAPTER ONE
Meet Jimmy

"They're coming up to the finish line!" said Jimmy. "And they're neck and neck! Come on, Big Al! Faster, Crusher, faster!"

Jets of flame shot from Crusher's exhaust and the robot racer surged forwards. Clouds of dust billowed up as Big Al pushed the giant machine into the lead ahead of Layla Jones and her racer, Aqua.

Layla launched Aqua straight into a shark-infested lake and the robot hurtled through the deep water like a torpedo. Big Al yanked on the steering wheel and Crusher swerved to avoid the water, taking a longer route through the forest. Crusher's razanium rotor blades whirred, hurling trees in the air like matchsticks as he crashed between branches. Big Al turned the wheel sharply to the right and his racer re-joined the track a split-second in front of Layla.

"Watch out!" cried Jimmy.

Suddenly Professor Plank and his robot, The Gadgetator, were on their tails. The professor threw a perfectly timed smoke grenade and a thick, black cloud smothered all three racers.

When the smoke cleared, The Gadgetator was in the lead. Jimmy held his breath as Big Al fired Crusher's jet engine one last time and pulled alongside The Gadgetator. Professor Plank began to release another smoke grenade, but before he had the chance, out came a sharp ramming-rod from a hatch on Crusher's side. It jabbed at the Gadgetator like a super-powered snooker cue and the robot swerved violently, spinning off the road into a ditch. Crusher roared towards the finish line.

"Did you see that? Did you?" shouted Jimmy.

"Of course I saw it," his friend Max replied. "I'm holding the phone you're watching it on! And we've seen it twice already this morning."

The two boys were stood in the school playground watching a re-run of the final round of the Robot Races Championship, their faces up close to the 3D phone screen as their heroes Big Al and Crusher sailed over the finish line. They yelled with joy as Big Al leaped down from his cockpit and punched the air, then they clapped as Crusher gently picked Big Al up in his massive robot pincers and swung him round in the air, bleeping and firing his boosters in triumph.

Every year a hundred million people around the world cheered on their favourite driver and robot racer as they competed for the ten million pound prize money. It was the biggest event in motorsport history and every boy and girl in the world dreamed of one day lifting the championship trophy.

On the screen, the picture changed and an advert came on.

"*Brand-New from Leadpipe Industries,*" bellowed a voice. "*Crusher toy with rotating crane pincers that* REALLY *work!*"

Jimmy and Max watched as the picture changed to the toy of The Gadgetator:

"*Available in four different colours!*"

There was even an action figure of Lord Leadpipe, the multi-trillionaire robot genius who had invented the Robot Races, with his bright red cheeks, long nose and monocle.

"I've got Crusher ... but which one should I get next?" Max asked. "Aqua? Or The Gadgetator?"

Jimmy sighed. He knew Grandpa would never be able to afford to buy him a robot racer toy.

"I'd love to go to the Robot Races Hall of Fame and see the *real* robot racers," Max continued.

Jimmy sighed even louder. *Grandpa* definitely *couldn't afford that*, he thought.

Jimmy had lived with his grandpa for as long as could remember. His parents had died when he was tiny and Grandpa had been looking after him ever since.

Living with his grandpa wasn't like being brought up by any normal old person. Wilfred Roberts didn't like watching daytime TV, or doing jigsaw puzzles, and he didn't tell Jimmy to wipe his feet or keep his hands off the best china plates. In fact, Grandpa was more of a big kid than Jimmy half the time. He was always making dens in the back garden, building home-made skateboards and letting Jimmy stay up with him until late at night, building campfires and toasting marshmallows as if they were on holiday.

When Jimmy was at school Grandpa worked really hard in his taxi, driving people around all day and sometimes half the night so that he could pay the bills and look after the two of them. But no matter how much he worked, they never seemed to have any money. Jimmy suspected it was because Grandpa was always giving free lifts to people with heavy shopping when it was raining, or to old ladies who couldn't afford the bus fare.

Jimmy and Grandpa were never hungry. But they ate a lot of jam sandwiches. They were never cold. But during the winter they usually put a coat on when they sat down to watch the telly. And when it was really cold they put on two coats and a hat.

"There are lots of people worse off than us, my boy," Grandpa would say.

Jimmy didn't mind being poor. He wasn't bothered that everyone else in school had a neat little 3D mediaphone while his clunky old phone was held together with sticky tape and only worked if you

11

tipped your head sideways and shouted. He didn't care that everyone else in school had the latest, whitest, shiniest trainers and plasma walls where they could watch eight hundred different TV channels and any film they wanted. He knew his grandpa was trying his best to make up for the loss of Jimmy's parents and he loved him for it.

But sometimes Jimmy did wish he could have just one robot racer toy.

He knew that if he really wanted one, Grandpa would go without food for a week to pay for it. But he didn't want to ask because if there was one thing that could take the smile off Grandpa's face, it was Robot Races. In fact, Grandpa *hated* the Robot Races.

Whenever Jimmy switched on the telly to watch them, Grandpa would start muttering to himself. His white fluffy hair would flop and even his huge white moustache would sag.

"What's up?" Jimmy would say.

But Jimmy knew what was the matter. As soon as Lord Leadpipe appeared on the screen to start the race, Grandpa would clench his teeth and start huffing and puffing crossly.

"Lord Leadpipe!" he would say, spitting the name out like it was a mouthful of sick. "He wasn't always a *lord*, you know. He used to be plain old Ludwick Leadpipe," he growled, punching a cushion and throwing it at the telly. "But he's always had the same stupid face."

"Shall I turn it off, Grandpa?" Jimmy would ask.

"Turn off your favourite programme?" he'd reply. "No, I won't make you do that!" And he'd leave the room, muttering as he went.

So whenever he got the chance, Jimmy watched the Robot Races with his friends.

"Let's watch it one more time," he said to Max.

"Again?" said Max. "The bell's going to go in a minute. And I'm not even supposed to have a phone in school."

"Just the end – the bit where Crusher rams The Gadgetator and wins," pleaded Jimmy.

But Max didn't reply.

Instead he was staring at the school gates. Something was heading across the playground. It was getting nearer. Nearer and louder.

With the roar of an engine and a squeal of brakes,

Horace Pelly arrived in a cloud of dust.

"What on earth...?" began Max.

"I bet you've never seen one of these before," said Horace with a big grin.

"That's the new Leadpipe F1-X Roboscooter!" Jimmy whispered to Max. "They're not even out yet! Not for another year!"

Horace was the school show-off. He had long, blond hair which he slicked back behind his ears and a handsome face like the kind of boy you'd see on TV selling breakfast cereal or chocolate bars. He had big, pearly white teeth that gleamed in the sunlight and smooth, tanned skin from the hundreds of holidays he went on with his family. And he *always* had the latest stuff.

Horace's dad was a very rich man. He worked with Lord Ludwick Leadpipe and was always giving Horace the latest prototype equipment from the Leadpipe laboratories to try out. Horace had been the first person in school with the Leadpipe Skatotron skateboard, the first one with the Leadpipe Multisport Pop-Up-Super-Stadium, the *only* one with the Leadpipe Digital Robocopter – you name it, Horace had it.

Jimmy was used to everyone else having more gadgets than him, but the worst thing about Horace was that he liked to make fun of people like Jimmy because they didn't have the same cool stuff as him.

Once, Jimmy had been walking down the street when he was caught in a rain shower and Horace and his dad had driven past in their brand-new Thunderbolt T1000 sports car. "Oi! Jimmy!" Horace had shouted. "Where's your car? I'd call a taxi, if I were you. Oh, yeah, that's right, your crummy old car *is* a taxi!" And with that, he and his father had thrown their heads back and laughed as they sped off into the distance.

A crowd began to gather around Horace and his scooter.

"I'd like you all to meet Steve," said Horace.

"Steve?" asked Jimmy.

"That's his name," said Horace, pointing to his scooter. "He's a Special Terrain Endurance Vehicle. Or S-T-E-Ve for short. Say hello, Steve."

"Hello, Horace. What can I do for you?" said a strange, metallic voice.

"He can talk." Jimmy was dumbstruck. "I thought only the robot racers had personality technology."

"Well, of course he talks," said Horace. "And that's not all! Steve? Activate auto-wheelie!" he ordered.

"Right away, Horace," said the motorscooter, revving up his engine. Then he raced off, reared up onto his back wheel and circled the crowd before returning to Horace. Everyone clapped and cheered.

"He's got all the extras," Horace boasted, pointing to the switches, dials and screens on the motorscooter's full dashboard. "Robonavigation ... autopilot ... a homing device if you get lost, of course ... and this is my favourite." He grinned. "Activate fridge, Steve."

"Right away, Horace," the scooter replied and, as if by magic, the dashboard flipped forward.

"The fridge for my packed lunch. And a few cans of ice-cold Orangiblast. Anyone want one?" Horace looked around.

Jimmy stayed silent as Horace handed out the cans of Orangiblast to his friends – the boys who made the loudest 'Ooh' and 'That's-amazing' and 'I'm-really-jealous' noises.

"Oh, and one more thing," said Horace. "He does this. Steve? Transform!"

16

With a gentle whirring noise, the scooter split in half, stretched in about six directions at once, and stopped with a quiet clunk. The scooter had turned into a quad bike.

The crowd stared, open-mouthed.

"Quite good, isn't it?" Horace smirked. "Dad says when I'm old enough to compete he'll get me a proper robot racer so I can win the Championship – but I suppose this will do for now. Who wants a ride?"

Everyone jumped up and down and waved a hand in the air – everyone except Jimmy.

Horace flicked a switch and started up the engine. It purred and hummed. "Why don't you all get in a queue and I'll take you on a lap of the playground," Horace said, beaming as everyone squabbled their way into a line. "Except you, Jimmy," he added. "I don't want you on my brand-new F1-X Roboscooter in those trainers. You'll make it all dirty."

Jimmy's freckly face went bright red. He wanted to say, "I don't care about having a ride on your stupid scooter." But instead he just scuffed the ground with his foot, making his trainers even dirtier.

Horace revved his engine and then hit the gas and

drove straight at Jimmy. "Out of my way, losers!" he shouted as he roared to the other end of the playground. Jimmy had to jump to one side, nearly landing in a huge, muddy puddle.

Horace couldn't get any more annoying if he tried, Jimmy thought crossly.

But he was wrong.

Horace braked sharply and turned in a tight circle. The engine purred powerfully. He looked down at the dark puddle in front of Jimmy and a nasty grin spread across his face. He hunched over his handlebars, revved the engine again and then accelerated.

Vrroooooommm!

The quad bike rocketed towards Jimmy, the deafening noise of the engine ringing around the playground. At the last second Horace wrenched on the handlebars and swerved, skidding into the water. The puddle exploded in a cold, muddy tidal wave which crashed down on Jimmy's head. Muddy water dripped from his hair, onto his eyebrows, down his nose and over his chin.

Jimmy closed his eyes and bit his lip. It was difficult to tell if the water in his eyes was tears or puddle water. He wiped it away with a soggy sleeve.

Horace pointed at Jimmy and opened his mouth. Jimmy waited for him to start laughing. But instead Horace's chin dropped and his eyes widened.

Instead of the laugh that Jimmy was expecting, out of Horace's mouth came a scream of terror.

"Aaaaarrggghh!"

CHAPTER TWO
An Announcement

"What?" said Jimmy, as Horace yelled. "What is it?" Jimmy looked around. Everyone else was staring – but not at *him*. They were staring *past* him. Jimmy turned to look – and his mouth fell open too.

Above them, a vast black shadow was sweeping across the sky. It spread over the school field and across the playground – and it was coming straight for them! The sun disappeared and darkness fell as if the whole town had been swallowed up by a huge black cloud.

"Aliens!" whimpered Horace, stuffing his fingers in his mouth and sobbing.

Jimmy and Max looked nervously at each other.

Shaking and fumbling, Horace tried to start his roboscooter. "Start, Steve, start!" he stuttered. But Steve didn't seem to be listening.

All the other boys ran.

"Come on!" yelled Max, as he raced towards the school building.

But Jimmy was looking up at the sky – and smiling.

Through the darkness he could just see the outline of a giant machine. But it wasn't an alien craft. It had a huge gold letter L in a golden ring on the side of it, which could mean only one thing. It was Lord Ludwick Leadpipe's airship.

Jimmy had seen it on the telly hundreds of times, hovering above the Robot Races.

"They're dropping something!" squeaked Horace, jumping off Steve and running round in a small circle. "They're dropping bombs on us!" he shrieked.

Jimmy looked up. A swarm of black dots was falling like rain from the airship and hurtling down towards them. "It's not aliens," said Jimmy, starting to laugh. "It's Lord Lead—"

"They're going to fall on *me*!" screamed Horace.

He threw his hands over his head, ran behind Jimmy and cowered.

"Look!" Jimmy gasped. "They're slowing down!"

He watched in amazement as the black dots seemed to fall in slow motion. One of them floated down in front of him and landed gently on the ground. It was like a shiny black snooker ball. The little orb started shaking – and then with a *pop!* it rose up on a pair of robotic legs.

His face frozen in terror, Horace peered over Jimmy's shoulder, watching as the ball started walking towards them.

"Mmffgllggfff!" said Horace.

"What?" said Jimmy, wishing Horace would shut up and get off.

"Grsffla inflayunnn!"

"Eh?" said Jimmy, staring in amazement as a pair of robot arms popped out of the sides of the little marching black ball.

"I said," shrieked Horace, "it's an invasion! We're under attack! Run!"

He kicked his roboscooter out of the way and ran, ducking and darting between the falling robots. But everywhere he ran, the black balls were cracking open and turning into little marching robots: legs first, then arms, then a head, and finally a voice.

"Gather round, gather round," said the little robot in front of Jimmy. "News from Lord Leadpipe."

Horace stopped running and turned around. "L-L-L-Leadpipe?" he stammered.

"Lord Ludwick Leadpipe is proud to announce a new season of Robot Races," the machine continued.

"Wow!" said Jimmy.

"And for the first time ever," it went on, "the Races will be just for children. If you're under the age of sixteen, then *you* can enter the Robot Races Championship."

With that, the little robot split in half, fired a shower of paper into the air, shrank back into a ball and rolled away to repeat the message somewhere else.

The great airship thundered into the distance as pieces of paper fluttered to the ground around Jimmy and Horace.

Jimmy reached out and grabbed one. "Look!" said Jimmy. "It's a leaflet about the new Robot Races!" He read it out, his voice shaking with excitement. "*I, Lord*

Leadpipe, am proud and delighted and honoured to announce this special season of Robot Races! A round of qualifying races will be held in every corner of the world, starting just two weeks from today. Only the six very fastest qualifiers will get through to compete in the Championship! So if you've got what it takes to win the most exciting race on Earth, and you're aged under sixteen and have your own robot..."

Jimmy's voice came to a croaky halt. Grandpa didn't have enough money for a *toy* robot racer, let alone a real one. The bubbles of excitement in his stomach all suddenly popped and he was left with the feeling that he'd eaten a bucketful of cold custard.

"Gimme that!" said Horace, snatching the leaflet out of Jimmy's hand. He read it quickly before pulling his phone out of his pocket and hitting a couple of buttons. Then he jammed the sleek device to his ear. "Dad? I need a robot. Lord Leadpipe has ... Oh, you've heard already. You've done what? Good. Bye."

Horace grinned at Jimmy.

"My dad knows about the Races already. He works for Lord Leadpipe, you see. And he's already been on the phone to NASA—"

"NASA?" asked Jimmy.

"Yes, NASA." Horace sniggered. "The people who build the robo-spaceships. My dad said Leadpipe robots aren't allowed in the competition, so he's ordered NASA to build my robot. I mean, how do you expect me to win the Robot Races Championship if I don't have the very best robo-technology that money can buy?" Horace's grin stretched even further. "What a shame you have absolutely no chance of entering the races. If your grandpa can't afford to buy you a decent pair of trainers, I don't think he'll be ordering a new robot from NASA!" Horace threw the leaflet in Jimmy's face. "Never mind, Jimmy," he added. "You'll still be able to enjoy watching me on TV, winning the Races. You have got a TV, haven't you?"

Jimmy didn't reply. He was watching Lord Leadpipe's airship sail away into the distance. He picked up the leaflet and looked at it one last time before crumpling it into a ball and stuffing it miserably into his pocket.

CHAPTER THREE
The Plan

It was starting to get dark as Jimmy headed for home. He could feel the crumpled leaflet at the bottom of his pocket, along with the jam sandwich Grandpa had made him for lunch. It only had one bite missing – and he hadn't even been able to swallow that.

Even the sight of Grandpa's black cab parked outside their cosy little house didn't cheer Jimmy up like it usually did. All he saw was the rust on the taxi and the broken garden gate and the front door held together with sticky tape.

Why is Grandpa home from work so early, Jimmy thought as he stepped into the hallway. *I hope he's not confused one of his passengers for a celebrity again and invited them home for a cup of tea.*

Only the other week, Jimmy had arrived home to find a scared-looking young gentleman nervously sipping a cup of Grandpa's home-made nettle tea. It had taken Jimmy half an hour to convince Grandpa that the accountant, who happened to be called Terry, was not in fact Leonardo Del Sanchez, the internationally famous actor and star of the movie *Space Encounters*.

"Oh dear," Grandpa had said. "Well, it was a pleasure to meet you anyway, my friend."

And with that, the poor accountant had seen himself out the front door, picking bits of nettle painfully from his teeth as he went.

"Grandpa! I'm home!" Jimmy called as he walked in. He pulled the leaflet out of his pocket and headed for the kitchen bin. "Hello!" he called again. Still there was no answer.

Jimmy found Grandpa sitting in the kitchen with his head in his hands, his wild white hair standing on end as though he had been trying to pull it out.

"Grandpa?" said Jimmy quietly.

Grandpa threw his hands down on the kitchen

table, looked up and tried to smile his usual smile. Instead his moustache slowly sagged until its two straggly ends met below his chin.

"What's up?" asked Jimmy. "What's happened?"

"I've had a letter," said Grandpa.

"A letter?" said Jimmy, starting to feel anxious.

"From my boss," said Grandpa. "The head of Total Taxis." Grandpa sighed and began to read it aloud. *"Dear Mr Roberts ... blah blah blah,"* he went on, *"thank you very much for all your hard work, blah blah blah ... with great sadness we confirm that your employment with us will end, blah blah blah ... and we wish you a happy retirement."*

Grandpa stared at the letter for a moment, and then his head fell forward and landed on the kitchen table with a thump.

"Retirement?" said Jimmy. "They can't *make* you retire – can they?"

"They can," said Grandpa, his voice muffled against the tablecloth, "and they have. I gave that company the best years of my life!" He sighed again, even more heavily this time, and slowly lifted his head off the table. "When I think of some of the people I've had in the back of that taxi … did I ever tell you about the time when I took Sidney Sharp from Marble Arch to Catford? He was the world's biggest film star back then – it was just after *Robomutants 3* came out. Did I ever tell you what he said to me?"

"Yes, Grandpa," smiled Jimmy. "A few times."

Grandpa's head fell forward again and his eyes sank shut.

Jimmy couldn't really understand how Grandpa ended up being a taxi driver – or why he loved it so much. As far as Jimmy could see, Grandpa was a genius. He could do maths faster than a calculator. He could do two crosswords at the same time – one with each hand – and finish them both in less than sixty seconds. Last year, the telly had burst into flames just three minutes before the Robot Races final was due to start. Grandpa had put the fire out and got it working again with nothing more than the spring out of an old ballpoint pen and a paper clip. Jimmy hadn't even missed any of the race.

Grandpa slowly got up and gave Jimmy a comforting pat on the shoulder. "Anyway, how was school? What's that you've got?" he asked, pointing at the screwed-up bit of paper in Jimmy's hand.

"Nothing," said Jimmy. "It's rubbish. I was just going to put it in the bin."

"Is it your school report?" Grandpa smiled. "Show me," he insisted, holding out his hand.

Jimmy handed it over. He knew what Grandpa would say.

Grandpa took one look at the leaflet and began to shake. "Robot Races?" he cried. "For children?" His face turned red and his moustache twitched. "Leadpipe!" he shouted, thumping a fist on the kitchen table. "That man is making millions and billions every year but it's still not enough for him!" Grandpa crumpled the leaflet and throttled it with both fists. "If I could get my hands on that man, I'd—"

But suddenly Grandpa stopped. He stared at Jimmy for a long moment, and then a grin spread slowly across his face.

Jimmy knew what that meant. Grandpa was having an idea.

After a long pause Grandpa whispered, "Would you like to go in for this Robot Race, Jimmy?"

"No," Jimmy lied, shaking his head. "No way! Why

would I want to do that?"

"Possibly because Robot Races is your favourite thing in the world ever." Grandpa looked at Jimmy searchingly.

"No," said Jimmy. "I like watching them, but that's different. Driving in one of them would be much too—"

"*Expensive*," finished Grandpa. "You think you'd never be able to race because you'd need your own racer. I'm right, aren't I?"

"No," said Jimmy firmly. "Well, what I mean is..." he added quietly, "yes." And suddenly words started pouring out of his mouth. "Horace Pelly's dad is getting NASA to build him a racer but he has everything he ever wants and his dad works for Lord Leadpipe and he gets paid thousands and thousands of pounds and we couldn't afford to buy a racer even when you had a job and now—"

"Buy a racer?" cried Grandpa, standing up. "Buy a racer? Why would we want to *buy* a racer?" He started bouncing up and down, the ends of his moustache jumping in the air.

Jimmy watched as Grandpa's shaking hands

smoothed the Robot Races leaflet flat. Grandpa folded it carefully and stuffed it in his pocket. Then he grabbed the letter from his boss and crumpled it into a tiny ball. He threw it over his shoulder and it sailed into the bin.

"Follow me," said Grandpa, skipping to the back door, his fluffy white hair streaming behind him. "I've got a surprise," he called over his shoulder. "No!" he said, correcting himself. "I've got a *plan*!"

CHAPTER FOUR
Grandpa's Shed

Grandpa danced down the garden, skipping between the clumps of weeds and stinging nettles. Jimmy followed, anxiously wondering whether Grandpa had gone mad.

"Where are we going?" asked Jimmy.

"We've arrived," Grandpa announced as they reached the end of the tiny garden. Jimmy looked at the huge bush in front of them.

"At the hedge?" Jimmy asked.

"At the *shed*." Grandpa laughed. He reached into the bushes and started pulling them apart. "It's in here somewhere."

Jimmy watched for a second, then began helping his grandpa clear away the overgrowth. Sure enough, behind the forest was a shed. But not much of a shed. Its wood was rickety and rotting, and it looked like it could be knocked over by a stiff breeze. The only thing about it that looked sturdy was the enormous metal padlock on the splintered wooden door. "I didn't even know we had a shed!" Jimmy exclaimed.

Grandpa stood on tiptoes and peered through the grimy glass of the shed window. "Look!" he cried.

Jimmy tried to look through the window. "I can't see a thing," he said.

"Good," said Grandpa. "Ready?"

Jimmy watched in silence as Grandpa took off one of his shoes and shook a little grey key into his hand. Trembling excitedly, Grandpa turned the key in the huge padlock.

"Do you always keep that key in your shoe?" Jimmy asked.

Grandpa didn't answer. He was looking left, and right, and behind him, and even up into the sky. Jimmy looked up too, even though he didn't know what he was looking for.

"All clear," said Grandpa, pushing the door open, shoving Jimmy into the darkness of the shed and shuffling in after him. Grandpa stuck his head back out of the door, gave the garden one last inspection, then pulled the door quietly shut.

Jimmy stood in the darkness. "What's going on, Grandpa?" he asked anxiously, wondering if this was the kind of thing people did when they were having a nervous breakdown.

"Ssssh," said Grandpa. "I just need to find the ... Aha!"

There was a click and a blinding light filled the room. Jimmy shielded his eyes, squinting painfully into the brightness.

He opened his mouth to speak. But no sound came out.

Inside the shabby, run-down little garden shed, a wide ramp led down into a large white room that looked like some kind of underground laboratory.

"What ... what...?" stammered Jimmy as he shuffled down the ramp. "Where am I?"

"You're in my workshop," said Grandpa. "I haven't been here in years."

Around the walls, white worktops were littered with lumps of metal and plastic, with piles of wires tangled up like spaghetti. Above them, rows and rows of tools hung from hooks and, beside them, huge pieces of paper were pinned to the wall: hundreds of drawings of electrical circuits and strange shapes with blades and teeth and wires and labels and all kinds of calculations.

Right in front of Jimmy, there was a desk piled high with rolls of paper, books, folders, a row of neatly sharpened pencils and a shiny metal hand that looked like the glove from a suit of armour. With a quick wink, Grandpa clipped two wires to the base of the shiny metal hand on the desk and flicked a switch on a control panel. The hand clenched into a fist.

"Wow!" said Jimmy.

Grandpa wiggled the joystick on the control panel. The fist unclenched and the fingers of the metal hand wiggled, too, as though they were scratching an invisible itch.

"That's amazing!" said Jimmy. "What—? I mean, whose—? And how come there's a whole building under the garden that I didn't know about?"

"When I was younger," explained Grandpa, "I was what they used to call 'a bit of a whizz-kid'."

"What do you mean?" asked Jimmy. "What did you do?"

"I invented things," said Grandpa, smiling modestly. "Well, one thing in particular."

"What?" Jimmy stared at Grandpa.

"There it is!" said Grandpa, pointing at the roof.

Jimmy looked up. Grandpa was pointing at something moving across the ceiling. It looked like a biscuit tin on tank tracks. When it got to the edge of the ceiling it trundled slowly down the wall and onto the floor, whirring and humming to itself.

"It's still working!" cried Grandpa happily. "No wonder it's so tidy in here!"

"But what is it?" asked Jimmy.

"Just a little old-fashioned robot," said Grandpa. A little door opened in the top of the biscuit tin and a mechanical arm reached out. It seemed to be waving at Jimmy.

"A robot?" gasped Jimmy, his mouth hanging open in amazement. "A real one?"

"Yes, but it's pretty basic. Well," laughed Grandpa,

"it *was* the first one ever invented."

"You…" began Jimmy. "You invented the world's first robot?"

"Well, yes," said Grandpa. "Yes, I suppose I did."

"How come?" said Jimmy, fizzing bubbles of excitement rising in his throat. "Why didn't you tell me!"

"I'm telling you now," Grandpa said. "Many years ago," he began, settling on a wooden stool at the desk, "before I became a taxi driver, me and a friend of mine worked together, imagining and inventing all kinds of things which we thought the world might want or need."

"What kinds of things?" asked Jimmy.

"We were working on a highly advanced Lie Detector," explained Grandpa. "It could even tell if you were *going* to lie before you'd opened your mouth."

"Incredible!" said Jimmy.

"Ah, but there was a problem," said Grandpa. "My friend and I couldn't agree about the wiring of the biorhythmical transmodulation simulator. I thought I was right. He thought he was right."

"Who was right?" asked Jimmy.

"Who knows?" replied Grandpa. "We stopped working together. He went off in a huff and took our laboratory assistant with him."

"You had an assistant?" asked Jimmy.

"Yes," said Grandpa. "Name of Hector. Anyway," said Grandpa after a moment, "I carried on working on the Lie Detector and one day a man came to see me. He said he was from a secret department in the secret wing of the Secret Services."

"The Secret Services? You mean, like a spy?" said Jimmy.

"Sort of," said Grandpa. "He was in the technology and gadgets department. He had heard I was good with electronics and computers and he wanted me to work on a top-secret project."

"The Lie Detector?" asked Jimmy.

"No," said Grandpa. "A robot."

Jimmy looked down at his feet. The biscuit-tin robot was rushing round his trainers, whirring away and cleaning them with a brush on a stick.

"Yes, just like this little chap here," Grandpa continued, grinning down at the robot.

"The Secret Services wanted you to build a cleaning robot? Why?" exclaimed Jimmy in amazement.

"D'you know how much the Secret Services spend on cleaners?" asked Grandpa. "My robot would have saved them a fortune! And there were hundreds of other things they wanted robots for too. Things that they said were 'CLASSIFIED'. So they built me this laboratory in the shed and gave me everything I could possibly need."

"The Secret Services built this shed?" said Jimmy, grinning excitedly. "Unbelievable!"

"I designed this prototype and took it to show the people at the secret department in the secret wing of the Secret Services. We had a few teething troubles to begin with – like the time it ripped their carpet to shreds and ate all the chair legs. But with a few minor adjustments, my plans were finished and I was ready to build a new, improved version of this little chap," Granda said, patting the biscuit-tin robot affectionately on the lid.

"Did you build it?" asked Jimmy.

Grandpa shook his head sadly. "One night," he said, "I was lying in bed when I heard a noise outside.

I looked out of the bedroom window, but I couldn't see or hear anything. And in the morning, I came down to the shed and all my plans were gone. Stolen."

"Stolen?" gasped Jimmy.

"A week later," sighed Grandpa, "the man who I had once thought was my friend – the man who I had trusted with some of my greatest ideas – started his own company selling the world's first robot. He had stolen my plans and made his own robot. Within a month, he was a millionaire."

"Who was he, this friend of yours?" asked Jimmy.

"His name," said Grandpa, "was Ludwick Leadpipe."

Jimmy stared at Grandpa. "You mean – your friend," he said at last, "the friend you worked with and invented stuff with – was Lord Leadpipe? So that's why you hate him!"

"Me?" cried Grandpa. "I don't *hate* Ludwick Leadpipe. I *despise* him."

"I can't believe it," said Jimmy. "I can't believe Lord Leadpipe would do something like that."

"Neither could I." Grandpa sighed. "And that's why I haven't been in this shed for thirty years. I told the Secret Services I was changing my career, and two weeks after the first Leadpipe robot went on sale I got a job with Total Taxis."

"But why give up all this to be a taxi driver?" asked Jimmy.

"You know where you are with a taxi." Grandpa nodded solemnly. "You can rely on a taxi. They always come when you call. And they don't sneak into your shed at night and steal your finest invention." He stared at the ground and sniffed. When he looked up again, there was a steely glint in his dark eyes. "So," said Grandpa, "the time has come to put things right. We are entering you for the Robot Races."

"But ... but ... but you hate Robot Races, Grandpa," said Jimmy.

"Not any more!" cried Grandpa, picking up the robot and spinning it around. "This is our big chance! D'you think I *want* to spend my retirement drinking tea and weeding the garden? D'you think I'm going to let you miss the opportunity to compete in Robot Races?"

Jimmy stared at Grandpa in open-mouthed amazement. Had the old man gone crazy? "But I haven't even got a racer," he mumbled when he eventually got his mouth working.

"Don't you see?" said Grandpa. "I'm going to *build* you a racer! When are the qualifying races?"

"In two weeks," replied Jimmy. His insides were jumping up and down with excitement, but the rest of him couldn't move.

"Better get cracking then," said Grandpa, sharpening a pencil and spreading out a roll of blank paper. "You put the kettle on, and I'll design you the greatest robot racer the world has ever seen!"

CHAPTER FIVE
Grandpa Gets Busy

Jimmy stared into his soggy cereal. He always ate breakfast with Grandpa – porridge and mashed bananas for Grandpa, cornflakes for Jimmy.

But not today. Or yesterday. Or the day before that. In fact, Jimmy hadn't seen Grandpa for days. He'd spoken to him through the shed door. He'd left cups of tea on the doorstep. He'd stood outside and listened to the banging and clanking as Grandpa worked on his racer. It was the first thing Jimmy heard in the morning and the last thing he heard at night. It couldn't be long before the neighbours started complaining.

Jimmy was thrilled that his grandpa was building him a robot racer. But he was also a bit worried: a bit worried that Grandpa hadn't seen daylight for days, a bit worried that he was going to wake up and find it had all been a strange dream ... and a *lot* worried about driving a robot racer.

The day before, Grandpa's taxi had disappeared. In the morning it had been parked outside the house as usual. But that afternoon, when he'd got back from school, the taxi was gone. He guessed Grandpa had sold it to pay for the racer.

What if Grandpa does all this work and spends all our money building an incredible robot and I turn out to be a useless driver? Jimmy wondered. *What if I crash? What if I come last?*

It all made him feel a bit sick.

When he got to school that morning, the first thing Jimmy saw was Horace Pelly in the yard, talking loudly to his friends.

"The engineers at NASA are working very hard on

my racer," announced Horace. "My dad's told them it's only a week and three days until the qualifying race and it's got to be ready in time. My dad says he doesn't care what it costs as long as it's the best robot racer the world has ever seen. They're putting in all kinds of extras. I've got a rotograbber and jet-thrusters just like Crusher and lots and lots of other amazing gadgets, but they're so top secret I'm not allowed to talk about them."

Jimmy wandered past, trying not to look interested.

"Hey, Jimmy," called Horace's sneaky, smug voice behind him. Jimmy stopped and turned round. "Come over here," said Horace.

Jimmy froze, his freckly face glowing scarlet as it always did when he was feeling nervous. "Why?" he asked.

"I want to tell you about my robot racer," said Horace.

Jimmy shuffled over. "I know about your racer," he said. "I heard you the first time."

"Well!" huffed Horace. "I thought you'd be interested. But I suppose it must be very disappointing for you. I know I'd be *gutted* if I was too poor to buy my own robot and enter the race." He chuckled to himself.

Jimmy wanted to say something. He wanted to say, "My grandpa's building my racer. He invented the world's first robot and would have been a world-famous robotics expert if his friend, Lord Leadpipe, hadn't stolen the idea and made trillions of pounds out of it." But he didn't. He didn't say a word.

"Anyway," said Horace, turning back to the admiring faces gathered around him, "let me tell you a little bit more about my racer. My dad thought it should be green, but I said no, it's got be black. Shiny metallic black. With chrome trim and leather—"

The bell rang. Jimmy and Horace and everyone else wandered into school, Horace still chattering away about his racer.

"All right, Jimmy?" said Max as they sat down for registration.

Jimmy nodded. He tried to think of something to say, but he couldn't stop thinking about the qualifying race – and every time he thought about it, his stomach fluttered and his brain did a somersault.

After registration, Jimmy tried to concentrate on

his maths. Up at the front of the class, the teacher was writing out complicated sums on the board and saying something about long division and square roots. But all Jimmy could hear was Horace boasting at the next table.

"Do you know there are hundreds of qualifying races," Horace was saying. "They're taking place in the United Kingdom, France, America, Germany, Japan, Australia – all over the world, all at the same time, with the fastest in each country going through to the Robot Races finals. My racer will win the one in Smedingham by miles, and my father says that no one in the world will be faster than me. They might as well give me my place in the Championship now."

Jimmy let himself daydream about what it would be like to stand on the winner's podium at the qualifier, the crowd cheering, the press cameras flashing, the TV interviewers fighting to ask him questions.

"*Jimmy,*" they were shouting, "*is it true your grandpa built your racer?*"

But before he could answer, the dream was shattered by Horace's whiny voice.

"It's such a shame you can't take part in the qualifier,

Jimmy. I mean, obviously you wouldn't win because I'm going to be the winner, but it would be nice for you to have a go. Maybe you could get a pair of robot roller skates. Could you afford a pair of those? I might have an old pair I don't need any more ... You're welcome to borrow them." Horace sniggered and the others joined in.

Jimmy bit his lip. *I'd probably stand a better of finishing on a pair of roller skates than with Grandpa's robot*, he thought glumly.

At break time, he and Max found a quiet corner in an empty classroom so that they could talk about the Smedingham qualifier.

"I bet my dad would give you a lift," said Max, "if you want to go. You are going, aren't you?"

"I think so," said Jimmy casually. He wondered whether to tell Max the truth – but he couldn't quite believe it himself. What if he told everyone he was going to enter the qualifier and then he didn't? He'd never hear the end of it. So he decided to keep quiet.

Suddenly, in the distance, he heard a scream. He looked up.

"What was that?" he asked.

Horace was on the other side of the playground, lying next to his scooter and shouting for help. He was surrounded by his friends, all standing around smirking and doing nothing.

Jimmy looked at Max and the two of them ran over.

Horace was squirming on the floor, holding his leg and whimpering to himself. "I fell off my scooter," he whined, "and I think I've broken my leg!"

"I'll go and get a teacher," said Max.

"No!" shouted Horace, sitting up suddenly, then sagging down again. "Wait. Before you go, I want to ask you a favour. I'm not going to be able to drive in the qualifier next Saturday with a broken leg. Jimmy, would *you* be my substitute? Would you drive my brand-new robot racer for me?"

Jimmy stared at Horace in amazement.

"I—" he began, his mind racing. What would Grandpa say? "Really?" said Jimmy. "Do you really mean it?"

"*No!*" said Horace, jumping to his feet and laughing like a horse with whooping cough. "No, of course I don't mean it!" he jeered. "Got you, didn't I?"

He ran off and everyone else rushed after him.

Jimmy watched open-mouthed as they raced around the playground, laughing and shouting until they had to stop to get their breath back. Jimmy sighed, stuffed his hands in his pockets and went off to a quiet corner, the sounds of Horace's laughter following him all the way.

A week went by and still there was no sign of Grandpa – or Jimmy's racer. As he made his way down the street towards his school on Friday morning, the sound of banging and crashing from the shed getting and fainter and fainter in the distance, Jimmy began to wonder if working twenty-four hours a day was healthy for someone Grandpa's age. He was old enough to retire, after all.

"Grandpa, are you OK?" Jimmy had called through the shed door as he put a cup of tea and a jam sandwich down in front of it.

"I'm fine, my boy," had come the cheery reply.

"The qualifying races are on Saturday, remember." Jimmy had said to the shed door. There had been a moment's silence – and then the hammering and the clanking had started again.

As he stepped into the playground, Jimmy saw Horace and his usual group of friends standing by the main gate.

"NASA delivered my racer last night," Horace announced.

The crowd of admiring faces around him gasped. Even Jimmy wandered over to listen in.

"He's called Zoom because he's so fast. I was driving him round my garden – which is very big, as you know," Horace explained. "My dad says he had to pay NASA a fortune to get Zoom ready in time, but he's worth every penny. Who's going to come and watch the qualifying race to see me win? I expect the whole class will be there – except you, Jimmy. My dad says your grandpa's so old and blind and deaf he's not allowed to drive that old taxi any more. Will you have to get the bus? Can you afford it?"

Jimmy suddenly felt himself getting very hot. His cheeks flushed and he clenched his fists. "What if you don't win?" he asked through gritted teeth.

Horace stared at Jimmy for a moment. "Don't you

understand?" he said very slowly, as though he was talking to a simpleton. "My racer was built by NASA. Even a fool like you and that old man you live with should be able to work that out."

Jimmy felt like he was going to explode. He'd never felt this angry, and for once he stood up to Horace. "Your racer," he snapped, "was built by NASA. But it's going to be driven by an idiot."

And before Horace could say another word Jimmy spun round and stormed out of the school gates and headed down the street.

Jimmy ran all the way back home, straight through the house and into the garden where he plonked himself down on the broken old deckchair Grandpa liked to sit in on sunny days. He closed his eyes, fighting back the tears that were threatening to trickle down his face.

"Hello, boy! What are you doing home? School's only just started," asked Grandpa.

Jimmy looked up. Grandpa was standing in the

shed doorway, smoke billowing out from behind him, his hair pointing in every direction and a lop-sided grin all over his face.

"What's the matter?" asked Grandpa. "You look like you swallowed a rotten fish."

"I didn't swallow one," said Jimmy. "I just go to school with one."

"What are you talking about?" asked Grandpa.

"That boy at school called Horace." Jimmy replied miserably.

"Ah." Grandpa nodded. "Why don't you tell me all about it?"

"He's entering the qualifying race too, and he goes on and on about winning and he said stuff and…"

"Don't you listen to him!" said Grandpa sternly, pulling Jimmy out of the deckchair and giving him a big hug. "There's only one boy who can win that qualifier and he's the boy who's wiping his nose on my overalls right now."

Jimmy laughed.

"Here," said Grandpa, digging in his back pocket and bringing out a grubby, oil-spattered handkerchief. "Wipe your nose on that."

Jimmy took the rag and gave his nose a snotty blow.

"Now get yourself to the kitchen," Grandpa ordered, "and get the kettle on. If we've only got two days until the qualifier, we'd better get a move on!"

Jimmy froze. "Grandpa, the qualifier's tomorrow," he said softly.

There was a long pause before Grandpa spoke. "The qualifier's tomorrow?"

"Yes," said Jimmy. "Tomorrow. Saturday."

"You mean it's Friday today?" asked Grandpa in astonishment. "What happened to Thursday?"

"Thursday happened yesterday. Remember?" said Jimmy, prickly sweat beginning to gather on his skin. "And today's Friday and tomorrow's Saturday ... the day of the qualifier."

There was silence for a moment.

"Is there another qualifier next week?" asked Grandpa eventually.

Jimmy stared at Grandpa, then took a quick peek through the shed door which stood ajar. On the floor were piles and piles of metal, wire and car parts — parts that didn't look like they belonged on any robot racer Jimmy had ever seen.

Grandpa was smiling hopefully at Jimmy.

Jimmy shook his head. "No, Grandpa," he said frantically. "It's eight a.m. tomorrow at Smedingham high street ... or never."

Grandpa narrowed his eyes, and pinched his lips together. Then he nodded, walked into the shed and pulled the door shut.

The clanking and hammering started again, twice as loud and twice as fast.

CHAPTER SIX
Cabbie Gets Going

Jimmy woke up to find Grandpa standing next to his bed. It was barely light outside.

"What time is it?" mumbled Jimmy.

"Six o'clock," said Grandpa cheerily.

"Six o'clock!" grumbled Jimmy. "Six o'clock in the morning? What's going on?"

Grandpa smiled. His eyes were red, his face was pale and his usually wild white hair sat flat on his head. But his moustache was bobbing up and down excitedly. "Come with me," he whispered.

Still in his pyjamas, Jimmy followed Grandpa downstairs, through the kitchen, out to the garden and over to the shed. With every step, he felt more nervous. He could feel the goose bumps on his arms, and a shiver ran down his spine as Grandpa reached for the door handle.

As he stepped through from the natural light of the morning sun to the fluorescent glow of Grandpa's workshop, his vision blurred for a second. But as his eyes grew used to the brightness, he saw a huge lumpy plastic sheet with something big underneath it standing in the middle of the shed.

"Jimmy," said Grandpa proudly, "I'd like you to meet Cabbie." With a flick of his moustache and a flash of his eyes, Grandpa tugged the plastic sheet off Jimmy's new robot racer.

Jimmy stared at it.

'New' wasn't really the right word. For a while, he wasn't sure what he was looking at. It appeared to be Grandpa's taxi, but with dull grey, metal patches welded onto it. The longer Jimmy stared, the worse it got. The front of the taxi looked like someone had hit it two or three hundred times with a hammer. The roof of the taxi appeared to have three upside-down dustbin lids bolted to it. And where the back doors used to be, on either side was a tangle of pipes and wires and tubes.

"What do you think?" asked Grandpa excitedly.

Jimmy tried to think. He looked at the car. He looked at Grandpa. He looked at the car again.

I can't go outside in that! he thought, his heart sinking. *I'll be laughed out of Smedingham when it breaks down after twenty metres.*

He thought about sitting next to Horace Pelly on the start line with all the other children from school laughing at him. The image of Horace braying like an over-excited donkey made him shudder. He turned back to Grandpa, not quite sure what to say.

"I, er—" Jimmy began.

"Well, don't just stand there," said Grandpa, beaming. "Introduce yourself."

Jimmy looked sideways at Grandpa and wondered what he was talking about. For a second he thought that all those long hours locked away may have made Grandpa imagine things.

"Say hello to Cabbie!" Grandpa insisted, pointing at his creation. "He's fully programmed with an intelligence-compiling processor, so the more you talk to him, the more he learns."

"Has it got ... personality technology?" asked Jimmy nervously.

"Er ... yes, probably," replied Grandpa, smiling uncertainly. "And Cabbie is not an *it*," he added, giving Jimmy a pat on the back. "He's a *he*. So say hello to him."

Jimmy looked at the machine and coughed. "Hello, Cabbie," he said quietly.

They waited. Nothing happened, and Jimmy's heart sank.

"I don't understand it," said Grandpa, reaching for a screwdriver and chewing the handle thoughtfully. "He should have said hello back. Maybe he will when he's ready."

Jimmy looked disappointedly up and down his racer. He knew he shouldn't feel so let down. He couldn't expect Grandpa to build a racer like the real ones – they just didn't have the money. Grandpa was a genius – but he wasn't a magician.

"Right!" said Grandpa, clapping his hands and rubbing them together. "It's nearly seven a.m. The race starts at eight in Smedingham ... which doesn't give us long to get you ready. Come on, Jimmy," said Grandpa, heading out of the shed towards the house.

Jimmy shuffled after him.

"You make breakfast," called Grandpa, "while I find a nice surprise for you."

Jimmy tried to smile.

What next?

Back in the house, Grandpa disappeared into the cupboard under the stairs while Jimmy put the kettle on and made yet another plate of jam sandwiches. He was beginning to feel sick and his hands were shaking. He had been feeling nervous about the race, but now he'd seen Cabbie he was terrified.

What am I going to do? he thought. *I can't tell Grandpa that I don't want to drive that old rustbucket, not after all the hard work he's put in. I'll have to give it a go...*

But then Horace Pelly's horsey face crept into his mind again, the boy laughing himself to death and making fun of Jimmy in front of Max and all his friends.

Grandpa was now deep in the cupboard under the stairs, muttering to himself. Occasionally something would come flying out: an old Christmas tree, a broom with no bristles, a chair with three legs.

"Aha!" came his voice from the depths of the cupboard and Grandpa suddenly appeared in the kitchen doorway with dust and cobwebs strung from the corners of his moustache to his ears. He was holding a battered crash helmet. "This was mine when I was just seventeen," he said, carefully placing it on the kitchen table. "And now it's yours, Jimmy." Grandpa patted the crash helmet fondly. A cloud of dust and flakes of paint landed on Jimmy's jam sandwich.

"Thanks, Grandpa," said Jimmy with as much enthusiasm as he could find.

Grandpa placed the helmet ceremoniously on Jimmy's head like he was crowning the next king of the world.

"Come on then, Jimmy," said Grandpa. "Let's go and win that race."

"What about my breakfast?" asked Jimmy.

Grandpa looked at the kitchen clock. "No time!" he said. "You can eat jam sandwiches any day of the week, but you'll only get one shot at qualifying for the Robot Races. Come on!"

They hurried back to the shed. Grandpa opened Cabbie's door and Jimmy climbed in.

There were buttons, switches, levers and dials covering every centimetre of the dashboard, on the doors to his left and right and even over the roof above his head. Jimmy's eyes widened as he looked around. Cabbie might look like a scrapheap on the outside, but on the inside it was like being in the cockpit of a robo-rocket.

"How do I—" he began, looking up. But Grandpa had already climbed onto his rusty old bicycle and was pedalling furiously out of the shed door, heading for the main road.

"I'll see you at the finish line!" he called over his shoulder.

Jimmy glanced back down at the hundreds of buttons, knobs and levers that lined every inch of Cabbie. "But ... but I don't even know how to make it go!" he said to himself.

"Go?" said an excited electronic voice from somewhere behind the dashboard. "Of course! Why didn't you say so?"

From all around Jimmy came a whirring noise which grew higher and louder as the racer powered itself up. A red button was flashing right in front of Jimmy.

"Am I supposed to press this?" Jimmy asked nervously, not sure if he should expect an answer from the voice or not. There was no reply. Jimmy shrugged, then reached out a finger, took a deep breath and gently pressed the button.

"Whoopeeeeee!" cried the voice and, with a deafening roar, Cabbie lurched forward at an incredible speed, hurling Jimmy back into his seat. He just had time to do up his seat belt before they crashed through the shed doors, out into the garden, through the neighbour's fence and onto the road.

They bounced down the kerb and Jimmy had to turn the steering wheel sharply to avoid hitting the wheelie bins belonging to Mrs Cranky across the street.

"Come on," encouraged Cabbie. "Put your foot down. Do you want to be in this race or not?"

For a second, Jimmy's foot hovered over the accelerator pedal as he thought how crazy this all was. He'd never even tried to drive a car before and now he was at the wheel of a real robot racer.

"Here goes," he said. He squashed his foot to the floor and Cabbie's engine roared.

"AAAAAAAAAGGGGHHH!" Jimmy yelled as they exploded out of the shed.

CHAPTER SEVEN
The Qualifier

Jimmy gripped the steering wheel in terror as Cabbie hurtled along. They raced up the street to the top of Smedingham Hill, where he could see the rest of the city spread out beneath them.

The roads were lined with safety barriers and crowds of people were standing behind them, waiting for the race to begin. Even before he saw the crowds, Jimmy could hear them:

"...nine ... eight ... seven..." they shouted in time with the huge display board which hovered above the circuit.

Cabbie was picking up speed, the houses, cars

and trees becoming a blur as they whizzed past. Jimmy could make out seven other racers, all revving their engines and sending clouds of exhaust fumes billowing into the air. He was relieved to see that three of them looked a bit like Cabbie: old cars with various pieces of scrap bolted to them.

One of them looked like Jimmy's crash helmet: a dented black fishbowl on wheels. Another one was so tiny Jimmy couldn't see how anyone, even a kid, could fit in it. It was like a big skateboard with something resembling an egg box stuck on top. And then Jimmy caught sight of a robot racer shaped like a sleek, black sports car. The sun glinted off its smooth surface, almost blinding its competitors before the race had even started. And the only thing brighter than the shine from the racer was the big, white, horsey grin on the face of its driver – Horace Pelly.

That must be Zoom, Jimmy thought. *Horace was right. It does look just like a real robot racer.*

"...six ... five ... four..."

Maybe I should turn back. This was a stupid idea.

"...three ... two ... one..."

"Slow down, slow down," shouted Jimmy. "We're

heading for the start line!"

"*GO!*"

A deafening klaxon rang out and the spectators all cheered and whooped.

"Speed up, speed up!" cried Cabbie. "They're leaving without us!" He rocketed to the start line, overtaking all the other racers before they could get going. "We're winning!" shouted Cabbie as they sailed ahead.

Jimmy turned to look behind in amazement. Cabbie was right – they *were* in the lead.

"Yes!" shouted Jimmy, punching the air.

But as soon as he'd said it, the whirring of a powerful jet engine could be heard getting louder and louder. Then a long, smooth black bonnet pulled alongside, followed by a crystal-clear windscreen, a glossy chrome steering wheel and then the tanned, handsome face of Horace Pelly. Jimmy watched Horace rubbing his eyes in disbelief. He clearly couldn't understand how Jimmy had managed to get a robot racer.

But Horace's shock didn't last for long. He looked Cabbie up and down through the gleaming glass of his racer and then he pulled a face at Cabbie – the same face somebody pulls when they notice they've got a big lump of dog poo on their shoe. Horace shouted something that sounded a lot like, "Ner ner ner ner ner!" and then Zoom's engine roared as he accelerated into the lead. He opened up a gap of 10 metres, then 20 metres, then 30. And before you could say "NASA", he'd disappeared off into the distance.

Two more racers swerved around Cabbie, overtaking him with ease even though Jimmy had his foot pressed hard on the accelerator.

"Oh no!" Jimmy said. "They're so much faster than us. What can we do, Cabbie?"

"Well," said Cabbie, "you could change gear for a start."

"Erm, how do I do that?" Jimmy asked. "You haven't got a gear stick."

"See those paddles flashing on each side of the steering wheel? The one on the left changes down and the one on the right changes up. Pull the one on the right."

Jimmy quickly pulled on the gear paddle and heard a deep growl coming from the engine. Cabbie seemed to flex his mechanical muscles, then all of a sudden he flew forwards. Jimmy hunched himself down over the steering wheel and focused on the road ahead as they whizzed back past the two racers just in front of them.

"Eat my dust, soggy bonnets," Cabbie cried as they left them in their wake. "You see, Jimmy. We're going to win this race. Now, show me what you've got."

They entered a tricky section of the course with sharp bends and tight corners, but with Cabbie handling the braking and Jimmy controlling the wheel they flew onwards, with the tyres screeching and the wind whipping at the windscreen as they weaved left and right.

"We're doing really well," Jimmy said. "We've left the others behind."

"Of course we have," Cabbie replied. "We're robot racers, and that's what we do!"

In the distance they could make out the cloud of dust that billowed into the air behind Zoom's jet engine.

"We've got to catch Horace and Zoom," said Jimmy. "What should we do?"

"See the small red button with the picture of the flame on it?" Cabbie replied. "It's flashing. Push it."

"What does it do?" asked Jimmy.

"You'll see," replied Cabbie.

Jimmy pressed the small red button.

For a moment nothing happened. And then the world seemed to explode. Jimmy was pinned back against his seat as Cabbie accelerated so fast that his front wheels left the ground. Before he knew it, Jimmy was whooping with excitement. He was really doing it: he was really a robot racer. At school, he was just a shy, quiet boy who only had one proper friend, but out here he could see hundreds of people cheering for him. He could feel confidence whizzing through his body like petrol through an engine, causing his fingers and toes to tingle. He wasn't scared, he wasn't being laughed at. And he was in second place!

"Wow!" he cried. "We could actually win this, Cabbie!"

"Of course we can," said the robot. "We're gaining on them. They're—" Cabbie paused, checked, recomputed. "Yes," he said. "They're slowing down!"

"Why would they do that?" Jimmy asked. But

before Cabbie could reply, the answer became obvious. Horace had begun to show off.

Zoom's roof was folding away and disappearing. Zoom was going open-top! Jimmy could see Horace sitting casually in the driver's seat with one hand on the steering wheel, his hair flying in the wind. The other hand was waving at the crowd and a group of TV cameras that had gathered. A moment later, Horace was standing up and steering with one foot. The crowd were going wild.

Then Horace turned round and saw Jimmy. "I've won this race already, Jimmy Roberts. You haven't got a chance," he shouted above the roar of the engines. He dropped back down into his seat and twiddled a couple of knobs on the dashboard.

The motor on Zoom's roof whirred loudly but nothing happened. Horace punched three more buttons and the whirring started again, followed by a nasty *crrruuuunnkk!*

"No!" screamed Horace over the noise of the wind. "We can't reach top speed with the roof down! Zoom, do something."

"System malfunction," the robot replied. "Roof

pod not responding. Unable to override."

"Noooo!" Horace yelled again.

"This is our chance, Cabbie," Jimmy said excitedly. "Let's get them."

The race was on!

Zoom slowed to round a bend in the road. Jimmy swerved Cabbie wide and tried to fit through a gap between the black robot racer and the crash barriers, but he could see Horace gritting his teeth and moving across to squeeze him out of room.

"We're going to hit them!" yelped Jimmy.

"No, we won't," Cabbie shouted back. "Watch this." And before he knew what was happening, Jimmy felt the whole world tip sideways. Cabbie had thrown himself onto two wheels.

"Go, Cabbie, go," Jimmy cheered. They inched past Zoom and took the lead. Jimmy could see Horace thumping the steering wheel and shouting as they flew past.

Ahead of them stretched a long straight road and at the end of it a huge crowd was cheering the two leaders on. They could just make out a man standing with a chequered flag in his hands.

"Look!" cried Jimmy. "The finish line! Come on, Cabbie!"

"Hold onto your hard drive," Cabbie replied, then he threw himself back on four wheels.

Jimmy's heart was racing faster than Cabbie's pistons. Zoom and Horace hadn't given up yet though, and Jimmy could see them in his mirrors, dodging and weaving behind them. The jet engine whirred louder than ever and Zoom inched alongside.

And in front.

Then Cabbie took the lead by a whisker.

Zoom edged back ahead.

They were neck and neck.

The finish line raced towards them. Jimmy's foot was flat to the floor, his grip on the steering wheel steady and solid, his eyes fixed on the chequered flag just a hundred metres away.

"Go! Go! Go!" Jimmy shouted.

"Faster, you useless heap of space junk!" Horace shrieked above the noise.

"This is gonna be tight," Cabbie said.

With a *whoosh!* they hurtled past the chequered flag as the crowd screamed their appreciation.

"Did we win? Did we win?" asked Jimmy.

But before Cabbie could answer, a huge crowd of people surrounded them, cheering and screaming and chanting.

"We did! We did!" yelled Cabbie, his lights and sensors flashing madly as he slowed to a stop in front of the grandstand.

Photographers and TV cameras pushed their way through the crowd. Reporters shouted questions.

Even louder than the crowd, a voice echoed from the loudspeakers: "Let's hear it for our winners ... *Jimmy Roberts and Cabbie!*"

The crowd went even more wild.

I don't believe it, Jimmy thought to himself. *We've won a Robot Race!*

Head spinning and feet stumbling, he climbed out of Cabbie's cockpit and into the crowd. From the corner of one eye, he saw Horace get out of Zoom, slam the door, kick it, and stomp off into the distance. He could just hear him shouting, "Dad! Dad! Get over here! I want that result changed right now. He cheated and it's not fair. He broke my roof, I know he did. *Do something!*"

Just then two figures pushed their way through the crowds towards Jimmy. It was Grandpa and Jimmy's friend Max, jostling with the scrum of photographers and the TV cameramen who were fighting to get the best picture. When Grandpa reached Jimmy, he seemed to be lost for words. But he had a grin on his face that was so broad it nearly split his face.

"We did it, Grandpa!" said Jimmy. "We won!"

"*You* did it, my boy," corrected Grandpa, crushing Jimmy in a huge hug. "*You* did it."

"Jimmy ... how did you...? Why didn't you...? When did you get a robot racer?" asked Max, his mouth opening and closing like a fish on dry land.

"Didn't I tell you my grandpa was an inventor?" replied Jimmy, trying to look cool. But he couldn't help the grin that spread across his face as Max high-fived him.

"You were awesome," Max said. I've never seen a race like it – and I've seen every Robot Race there's ever been!"

Just then, the crowd surged around them, and before Jimmy could say anything else to his grandpa or best friend, he was being carried away on a tidal wave of jostling bodies, swept towards a podium where a camera was pointing right at them. Behind the camera was a huge blank video screen.

"Ladies and gentlemen," boomed a voice from the loudspeakers. "Please wait as we calculate the results of the qualifiers from all around the world."

The video screen flickered into life. Numbers and names flashed up, whizzing by and whirring, as the results from the hundreds of qualifiers were beamed in. Jimmy held his breath. He had won the qualifier in Smedingham – but surely he wouldn't be one of the fastest racers in the world?

"Remember," echoed the voice, "only the six fastest qualifiers will win a place in the Robot Races Championship. And ... the ... results are ... in!"

The screen went blank for a moment before it flickered and an image appeared. It was a face: the round, red face of Lord Ludwick Leadpipe, his monocle gleaming and a beady black eye peering through it.

"The results of the qualifiers are as follows—" announced Lord Leadpipe. He paused and checked his notes, cleared his throat, scratched his ear, and cleared his throat again. The crowd was absolutely silent, leaning forwards in their seats as they waited.

"With the fastest qualifying time in the world, in first place," said Lord Leadpipe, "from the United States of America, Chip Travers and his racer, Dug."

Lord Leadpipe's face disappeared, and in its place appeared the face of an African-American boy in a baseball cap, whooping and screaming on top of a huge yellow and gold robot shaped like a digger. The crowd cheered.

"In second place," announced Lord Leadpipe, "from Japan, Princess Kako and her racer, Lightning."

The face of the bouncing boy in the baseball cap vanished and a solemn Japanese girl appeared, leaning against a motorbike racer. Princess Kako smiled and nodded gently at the camera as she received her round of applause.

"In third place," said Lord Leadpipe, "from Australia, Missy McGovern and her racer, Monster."

A red-haired girl filled the screen suddenly. She was sat comfortably on the giant wheel of her monster truck racer, giving a big thumbs-up to the camera.

"In fourth place," said Lord Leadpipe, "from Egypt, Samir Bahur and his racer, Maximus."

More cheers rang out. Now it was the turn of a serious-looking boy to look out from the giant screen. The boy was scowling at the camera, and it was hard to believe he'd just won the race of his life. Behind him was an impressive hovercraft racer with giant fan engines that looked like they'd been taken straight from a windmill.

"In fifth place," said Lord Leadpipe, "from Sweden, Olaf Trygvasson and his racer, Velocitron."

The screen showed a stocky figure in a leather jacket, his head encased in a huge black crash helmet. He waved at the camera.

"And finally, in sixth place, from the United Kingdom—"

The crowd fell deadly silent.

"Jimmy Roberts and his racer, Cabbie," announced Lord Leadpipe.

Jimmy stood stunned. There on the screen was a pale, skinny blond-haired boy with freckles all over his face and a mouth that was hanging open in surprise.

It's me! Jimmy thought.

From somewhere in the background he could hear Lord Leadpipe continuing, "And that's the end of the qualifying rounds. Thank you all for watching, racing fans. Tune in next time to see how our six contestants get on during the first round of this special edition of the Robot Races Championship. Bye for now." And with a wink to the camera through his monocle, the cheery face of Lord Leadpipe disappeared.

"Woo-hoo!" yelled Grandpa.

"You did it!" cheered Max.

I must be dreaming, Jimmy thought. *I can't really have qualified for the Robot Races Championship, can I?*

CHAPTER EIGHT
Meeting the Competition

The next day, at exactly 8.57 a.m., Jimmy and Grandpa made their way outside as the sky above them darkened. Lord Leadpipe's giant airship floated gently overhead, blocking out most of the sun and making it seem to Jimmy like it was still night time.

Cabbie drove out of the shed and parked himself in the garden. "How do I look, Jimmy?" he asked.

Jimmy squinted at his racer. Grandpa had smartened up Cabbie's appearance and made him look much more like a professional robot racer, but there were still grey patches welded onto the old taxi chassis, and lumps and bumps hammered into the bonnet. Cabbie wouldn't be winning a beauty contest any time soon.

"You look amazing," said Jimmy, hoping that he sounded convincing.

Jimmy and Grandpa packed a suitcase of clothes and Grandpa's toolbag safely into Cabbie's boot before climbing into the front seats. Jimmy looked around Cabbie's cockpit. There were even more buttons and levers and switches than he remembered. Grandpa had spent half the night underneath Cabbie, making modifications and saying all the time, "Things are only going to get tougher from here on in, my boy. So I want Cabbie to be prepared for any situation. Who knows what that scoundrel, Leadpipe, will have planned for you?"

Before Jimmy could investigate the dials and knobs any further, there was a *boom!* which shook the earth as a huge platform was lowered from the airship on thick, metal chains.

"Amazing!" said Jimmy.

"Incredible!" Cabbie added.

"Show-off," Grandpa muttered under his breath.

The platform reached the ground and Jimmy drove

Cabbie up onto it.

Grinding and creaking, the chains were winched up again and Jimmy peered over the edge of the platform as they rose higher and higher into the sky. The platform climbed above the trees, above the tops of the houses and kept on going until it was high into the clouds.

Grandpa had his eyes squeezed shut, and his skin had turned a nasty green colour, as though he might be sick at any moment. But for Jimmy, this was one of the most exciting moments of his life.

I can't wait to tell Max about this. I'm actually going to get to see inside Lord Leadpipe's private airship!

Finally they heard a loud *clunk* as the winch ground to a halt. Jimmy looked around at his new surroundings in amazement.

It wasn't like any airship Jimmy had ever seen before. Usually, an airship or zeppelin had just a small box for passengers slung under a huge balloon filled with gas. But in Lord Leadpipe's craft, the gigantic balloon was a completely solid structure – and it bustled with more activity than a shopping mall.

Everywhere Jimmy looked he could see people

rushing around carrying equipment or shouting orders over the sound of engines firing. There were electronic signs pointing to places like the "Swimming Pool", "Cinema" and "Restaurant". And the room they had been lifted into was actually the most enormous workshop Jimmy had ever seen. It was bigger than a cathedral. Under brilliant white spotlights the mechanics and pit crews for each of the racers worked on their robots, sending showers of sparks and jets of steam and billows of smoke up to the roof. None of them even seemed to have noticed Jimmy, Grandpa and Cabbie make their entrance.

As they opened Cabbie's doors and climbed out, Jimmy saw that the platform had lifted them directly into their own workstation, with shelves, cupboards and tool chests full to the brim with state-of-the-art gadgetry that made Grandpa's battered old toolkit look prehistoric. But before he could say a word, Jimmy felt a gentle tap on his shoulder. He spun round to see a tall man with huge eyebrows grinning at him. The man wore a dark blazer with a gold 'L' for Leadpipe on the breast pocket, a huge red cravat tucked under his pointed chin, and two tufts of cotton wool were poking out of his ears. Jimmy guessed this was to help block out the worst of the noise coming from the mechanics.

"Joshua Johnson," said the tall man in a loud voice. "Robot Co-ordinator. I'm in charge of looking after the teams during the competition, so if you have any problems, you see me, OK?" He grinned at Jimmy and Grandpa, his eyebrows doing an excited little dance as he offered his hand.

Jimmy shook it.

"And you must be..." Joshua Johnson pulled a clipboard from somewhere behind his back and stared at it for a moment. "Jimmy Roberts. Delighted!"

"This is my grandfather," said Jimmy, nodding at Grandpa. Joshua Johnson moved along to Grandpa and held out his hand.

"Joshua Johnson, Robot Co-ordinator," said Joshua Johnson again. Grandpa shook his hand and grinned.

"And this must be Ca—" said Joshua Johnson, peering over Grandpa's shoulder at Cabbie. "Oh," he said. He checked his clipboard again and squinted at Cabbie like he couldn't quite believe his eyes. "Is he...? Is he ... OK? I mean, has he had an accident? Will he be able to race?"

Jimmy felt his face going red. "Cabbie's fine," he said quietly.

"I'm more than fine," Cabbie chipped in. "I'm great. Just wait until you see me race, Bushy-brows. I'll show the rest of these robots a clean pair of tyres."

Joshua Johnson looked a little flustered and he combed his giant eyebrows nervously with his fingers. "Right," he stuttered, trying to look as dignified as possible. "Come and meet the other racers."

He marched off towards a pit station where a group of ten or fifteen people stood, all dressed in black wearing black baseball hats, black trousers and black shirts. Each shirt had a streak of silver lightning zigzagging down the back.

"Excuse me, excuse me," said Joshua Johnson, edging his way through the mechanics. Jimmy and Grandpa followed him.

The crowd suddenly parted, and there, at its centre, was a pale, skinny Japanese girl in silver motorcycle leathers. She stared at them with huge black eyes.

"Your Highness, may I introduce Jimmy Roberts

and his grandfather from the United Kingdom?" said Joshua Johnson, bowing his head politely.

"Your Highness?" echoed Jimmy in surprise.

"Yes," said Joshua Johnson. "This is Her Imperial Highness, Princess Kako of Japan."

The girl bowed her head. Jimmy did the same.

"And this is Lightning," the robot co-ordinator said, waving a hand at a large, powerful motorbike with a silver lightning bolt painted on the fuel tank.

Jimmy had never seen a motorbike like it. Lightning had spoilers and exhausts sprouting from every part of his body, and his huge, shiny engine looked like it could have been used to power a jumbo jet rather than a lightweight machine. Lightning flashed his headlight in acknowledgement, stretching the tip of one of his spoilers and flexing a pair of turbo jets positioned on each side of the back wheel. He reminded Jimmy of a panther, stretching after a short nap.

Joshua hurried Jimmy and Grandpa along to the next station where there was even more noise and activity than at the last. This," said the co-ordinator, bowing and backing away, "is Missy McGovern and her racer, Monster, from Australia."

Joshua Johnson led Jimmy and Grandpa to a huge monster truck where a short, stocky girl in oil-stained overalls was standing with her hands on her hips.

"What's the point of your having self-regulating tyre pressure if I have to check it all the time, you useless lump?" she was shouting in a broad accent.

"Gives you something to do," said a metallic female voice from the tiny cab perched on top of the enormous chassis. "Stops you getting bored," it added.

Jimmy had seen pictures of monster trucks before, but standing up close to one for the first time made him realize just how enormous they were. Monster was at least four times as high as Cabbie and three times as wide. It was impossible to see what kind of gadgetry Monster had from down here, but Jimmy knew that the mammoth wheels alone could crush most of the competition.

"Maybe I'll send you to the scrappy and get a decent racer," continued Missy, kicking a huge tyre affectionately.

"That hurt!" said the metallic voice.

"Good," said Missy, stomping off towards her

engineers, who all wore matching oil-stained overalls.

Joshua Johnson grinned with embarrassment. "I'm sure she'll say hello later," he said, "when she's calmed down a little. And this," he went on, hurrying away, "is our next competitor..."

He led Jimmy and Grandpa over to a boy of average height with short black hair. His face looked like it had been carved in stone. "This is Samir Bahur and his racer, Maximus," said Joshua Johnson. "Samir, this is Jimmy Roberts from the United Kingdom."

Samir stared with his cold grey eyes and gave Jimmy a short sharp nod of his head. "I prefer to be known as Sammy," he said with a thick North African accent. Then, without another word, he turned away to Maximus, a futuristic hovercraft powered by two hoverblades.

His mechanics were scurrying around in khaki overalls, checking over every inch of the robot for problems. Barking orders at them was a broad-shouldered man with a thick, black beard who Jimmy vaguely recognized.

"That's Samir's father, Omar Bahur," whispered Joshua Johnson quietly. "He's a former Robot Races champion himself, and by far the scariest man I've ever met," he added even more quietly, before hurrying away.

That's where I know him from, Jimmy thought to himself. *I've seen old videos on Max's phone of Omar winning races.*

"There is one more competitor we'll be picking up on the way to the Grand Canyon," explained Joshua Johnson over his shoulder as they walked. "And one other competitor for you to meet now. He's from the UK too." Jimmy and Grandpa followed Joshua Johnson towards a sleek, black, shiny robocar that looked worryingly familiar. Beside it, facing the other way, was a short, skinny boy with a big head. He was dressed all in shiny black leathers. The boy turned round and sneered a huge horse-teeth smile.

Jimmy stared in horror.

"Jimmy, this is—" said Joshua Johnson.

"Horace Pelly," Jimmy gasped.

CHAPTER NINE
The Return of Horace Pelly

"I wondered when *you'd* turn up," sneered Horace, looking at Jimmy as though he'd found him stuck to the bottom his shoe.

Jimmy said nothing.

"Pleased to see me?" said Horace.

Still Jimmy said nothing. His mouth seemed to have stopped working.

"These NASA people," said Horace, nodding over his shoulder at a small group of men and women in blue overalls and peaked hats, "are amazing. They've worked wonders with Zoom since the qualifier. He's faster, cleverer and better equipped. He's got thirty-two more features than—"

"But—" Jimmy started.

"Why am I here?" asked Horace, his mouth breaking into that sneer again.

Jimmy nodded.

"That Swedish boy? Olaf something?" said Horace. "Turned out he wasn't a Swedish boy at all – just a very short adult racing-car driver. He was disqualified. And I was the next fastest qualifier. So I suppose you could say—"

"Horace!" called a voice.

A tall, slim man marched up to them. He looked just like Horace, apart from the fact that his thick hair was jet black while his son's hair was blond, and he had a long, thin moustache which sat just above his top lip like someone had glued a pipe cleaner under his nose. His hair was slicked back and he wore a smart, expensive-looking suit.

"Yes, Daddy?" said Horace.

"Stop yabbering at this boy, Horace," said Mr Pelly, twiddling his moustache irritably between his finger and thumb. "Come with me. We must prepare for victory."

"But you're paying those NASA people to do that for us, aren't you, Daddy?" whined Horace.

"Not winning the race," laughed his father. "I mean, your victory *speech*. Remember: when you're on the winner's rostrum after each race, you must thank everyone who made your victory possible – but especially your beloved father, Hector Pelly. Oh, and you should probably say something about Mummy too, I suppose. Come along and we'll practise it."

And with that, Horace and his father marched off to a vast, silver motorhome parked behind Zoom. The door slid open automatically, and the Pellys disappeared inside.

"Disqualified!" exploded Grandpa in disgust when they'd gone. "There's something funny going on here."

"What do you mean?" asked Jimmy.

"If that boy got in the finals fair and square, Jimmy lad," hissed Grandpa angrily, "then I'm a milkmaid!"

"You mean—?"

"I mean," said Grandpa, "that his father has paid someone a lot of money to get him in this race – and it's probably something to do with that no-good, double-dealing, cheating snake, Ludwick Lead—"

"Ssshhh!" hissed Jimmy. "Lord Leadpipe's probably on the airship. He'll hear you!"

But there was no need for Grandpa to hush. A voice boomed out of the loudspeakers above their heads and silenced everyone.

"Ladies and gentlemen," it announced, "we have one more competitor joining us, and then we'll be landing at the Grand Canyon racetrack within one hour."

Everyone cheered.

"Well," said Grandpa, "that was quick! Six thousand miles at hyperspeed, and not a whisper of turbulence!"

"Are you impressed with Lord Leadpipe's airship?" asked Jimmy.

"No," replied Grandpa quickly.

Jimmy smiled.

A few seconds later, there was a terrific grinding and whirring noise and the platform on which Cabbie and Jimmy had been lifted up to the airship was lowered down to the ground again. It soon returned with the huge yellow digger that Jimmy had seen on TV just a couple of days before. Five or six mechanics in yellow overalls were now perched on the beefy caterpillar tracks Dug used instead of normal wheels. From its driver's cab a boy waved cheerfully.

"Hi! You're Jimmy!" he yelled in a broad American accent. "I saw your picture in the papers. I'm Chip Travers. How are you doing?"

"Fine, thank you!" replied Jimmy cheerfully.

"This here's my pa," called Chip, pointing at the man sitting next to him. "And this," said Chip, patting the digger's dashboard, "is Dug. Say hi to Jimmy, Dug!"

Dug swivelled his digging arm round to Jimmy. He jumped backwards as it swung at him.

Chip laughed. "He don't bite!" he called.

Jimmy edged forward and held out his hand. Ever so gently, Dug grabbed Jimmy's hand in his giant arm and shook it up and down.

"See?" called Chip, jumping down from his cab and shaking first Jimmy's and then Grandpa's hand.

* * *

Jimmy felt like he was in a daze. Just twenty-four hours before, he'd been a nobody. But now he'd done interviews with newspaper reporters, signed autographs, stood for millions of photos and hitched a ride on Lord Leadpipe's airship with the best robot racers in the world.

Jimmy looked over at Grandpa, who was making a few last-minute improvements to Cabbie. "Right. That's all the rocket-boosters supercharged and tightened." Grandpa grinned. "Now, what's next?"

Just at that moment a voice chimed in over the loudspeaker.

"Ladies and gentlemen, if you move to the viewing area, you will see the Grand Canyon and the race circuit where we will soon be landing."

There was a rush to the row of windows on the far side of the airship. Jimmy and Grandpa managed to squeeze in between Chip Travers' dad and one of Sammy's mechanics to get a view over the Grand Canyon and the new racetrack that had been created by the secretive race-builders. They all gasped.

"I've been to the Grand Canyon more times than I care to remember," said Chip's dad, "but I've never seen it from up here. Wow!"

Looking down from the airship, the Canyon was like a huge crack in the dusty red desert, shelves of red rock shimmering in the heat of the afternoon sun. There were no smooth roads to drive on, or soft tyre walls to protect the racers from getting damaged. There were just sheer cliffs and solid rock walls, steep hills to climb and slippery slopes to tackle on a racetrack which wound down, through and round the famous landmark.

Everyone aboard the airship stared in silence as the ground came nearer and the Canyon grew larger in the window.

A few minutes later, Jimmy, Grandpa, Cabbie and all the others were safely on the ground. As they made their way to the start line they could see thousands of fans making their way up to the grandstands dotted around the circuit. They scrambled over the Grand Canyon like ants over a fallen tree, all dressed in brightly-coloured clothes. Some were carrying banners and flags – Jimmy even saw a few Union Jacks waving in the breeze and his heart skipped a beat as he thought of all the people who would be cheering him on both here and back at home.

Above them camerabots and safetybots hovered, darting among the vast display boards that floated over the racetrack. Some of the boards were counting down the last few minutes to the start of the race while others showed a video of the racecourse layout. An announcer was explaining the different challenges that the drivers would face, but Jimmy couldn't understand a word that was being said. His mind had gone fuzzy and as he looked along the line of racers he suddenly he felt very cold and very sweaty.

Come on, Jimmy. Pull yourself together, he told himself.

Once the racers were positioned on the grid, the mechanics swarmed over their vehicles once more to perform final checks while the competitors prepared themselves for the race. Horace Pelly came over, sneering his usual sneer, but now dressed in a specially-made white racing outfit with a red stripe down the arms and legs.

Jimmy looked down at his own racing outfit: jeans, a T-shirt and a battered helmet that was probably decades old. He swallowed hard.

"I see you're admiring my outfit," sneered Horace. "My dad had it invented specially. It's lightweight, titanium-lined Cryothonix™. Fireproof and crashproof. My dad says I'm too precious to risk anything less. You're going with those tatty jeans and grubby T-shirt, I suppose?"

"Well, I'm not planning on crashing or catching fire," muttered Jimmy. He hated how Horace always made him feel. He might have beaten him in the qualifiers, but Horace still treated him like a joke.

"And what modifications have you made to … to…"

"Cabbie?" said Jimmy.

"Yes, that old rust-bucket of yours," said Horace. "It's a tough terrain here. I hope you've prepared him for it. My NASA engineers—"

Jimmy turned away and tried to stop listening, but he couldn't help noticing that all of the other drivers were wearing custom-made racing outfits too. Jimmy looked more like he was going for a stroll in the park.

"Anyway," said Horace, interrupting Jimmy's thoughts, "I've wasted enough time talking to you. I must go and be interviewed by the press." Horace strode over to a group of reporters. Cameras started flashing as he posed and grinned.

Jimmy climbed into Cabbie's driver's seat and strapped himself in, before looking nervously at the expensive robot racers around him.

Zoom's black paintwork shone in the sunshine.

Dug reached out his huge hydraulic arm to high-five people in the crowd.

Towering above the others, Monster was blowing exhaust fumes high into the air.

Maximus the hover-bot revved his fan engines menacingly.

And right next to Jimmy and Cabbie was Princess Kako aboard her robocycle, Lightning, practising some moves. Lightning transformed at top speed from motorbike to robo-rocket and back to motorbike again.

Jimmy noticed that all of the other racers had the names of sponsors splashed across their sides. Zoom and Horace were supported by *Gleam Toothpaste – For a Winning Smile!* Lightning had the words *Tokyo. Pro.Robo.Co – by Royal Appointment* printed on his mudguards. Chip and Dug were sponsored by *Luke's*

Lasers – the Brightest and Best. The words *Cairo Construction* were splashed on the roof of Maximus; and Missy and Monster sported the title *Robotron Rocket Boots – Footwear that Flies!*

Grandpa had phoned Total Taxis to see if they wanted to sponsor Cabbie. They had said they would think about it and call Grandpa back – but they hadn't.

What am I doing here? Jimmy thought. *I haven't got a hope of winning this race.*

"All right, my boy?" said Grandpa, appearing from underneath Cabbie, where he had been making some final adjustments.

Jimmy stared sadly at the other racers.

"All right, Jimmy lad?" repeated Grandpa, louder this time.

"Yeah, fine," Jimmy replied quietly.

"They might look better than Cabbie," said Grandpa softly, "but they haven't got you at the wheel, my boy. Don't tell him I said this," Grandpa whispered, "but I know Cabbie's not the best-looking racer."

"I heard that," Cabbie said indignantly.

"But looks aren't everything, though." Grandpa continued, grinning so much that his moustache wobbled. "You wait till you're out there on the track. You'll see."

Jimmy nodded. He hoped Grandpa was right.

"Right!" said Grandpa patted Cabbie's bonnet. "I'm off to the first pit stop to get myself ready. I'll see you there!"

Jimmy watched Grandpa disappear into the crowd.

"Racers!" boomed a voice from the loudspeakers. "Take your positions!"

CHAPTER TEN
And They're Off!

"This is it," said Cabbie, giving himself a pep talk. "The big one. Time to make it count. When it really matters. Everything to play for…"

Jimmy chewed on his fingernails as he looked through Cabbie's windscreen down the start line.

"Cabbie looks like he's been in a fight with a garbage truck," he heard Horace shouting to Chip.

"It's a race, not a beauty contest," Chip yelled back.

In the blue sky above them Leadpipe's airship hovered. As they watched, Lord Leadpipe's jolly face appeared on an giant screen on its side, peering down at the contestants through his monocle.

"Ladies and gentlemen," he said, his big red face beaming and his voice ringing around the Canyon, "it gives me great pleasure to welcome you all to the first-ever Robot Races for under-sixteens. Today's race will see our drivers taking on the challenges of the incredible Grand Canyon and battling for the lead in the Robot Races Championship."

"Look at them all," said Jimmy sadly as Lord Leadpipe continued to warm up the crowd. "Dug and Monster and Lightning ... they all look so ... good."

"Yeah. Let's just give up and go home," said Cabbie.

"What?" Jimmy spluttered. "But ... it's the Robot Races! We can't quit now! I've wanted to do this my whole life..." He trailed off as he realized what Cabbie was trying to do.

"Exactly. Now, come on, Jimmy!" Cabbie yelled. "We're in this race, and we'll show those fancy, shiny robots how it's done."

"You're right." Jimmy gripped the steering wheel. "Let's show them what we can do."

Jimmy jumped as Grandpa's voice crackled out of

a little radio on Cabbie's dashboard.

"Everything OK, Jimmy?"

"Everything's fine, Grandpa," Jimmy said nervously.

"Everything's just peachy, Wilf," said Cabbie. "A-OK. Ticketyboo. Hunky dory. Couldn't be better. So let's get this show on the road."

"ON YOUR MARKS...!" yelled Lord Leadpipe suddenly.

Jimmy looked for the ignition button. Then looked again. A cold shudder ran through him and he desperately started searching the panel in front of him.

"It's gone!" he cried.

"What's gone?" said Grandpa and Cabbie together.

"The big red ignition button. The thing that makes us go! Where is it?" Jimmy said, starting to sweat.

"GET SET!" Lord Leadpipe's voice echoed around the racetrack. The other racers' engines filled the air with a rumbling roar.

"Oh," said Grandpa, as though he had just remembered something. "Sorry, lad, I meant to tell you. I did move some of the gadgets around. One or two last-minute, ahem" – he coughed – "adjustments."

"I've got it!" shrieked Jimmy, pressing a red button on Cabbie's ceiling.

"*GO!*" Leadpipe bellowed.

With a click and a rush of air, a hatch in Cabbie's roof flew open and an enormous magnet on a length of chain shot up to the sky. It came clattering down about thirty metres from the car, narrowly missing an elderly spectator and his dog.

Zoom, Dug, Monster, Lightning and Maximus all roared into the distance, covering Cabbie's windscreen with a cloud of dust.

"I think that's the wrong button," Grandpa said helpfully.

"What do I do? What do I do?" said Jimmy.

"Don't panic!" Cabbie said. "I'm making the ignition button flash."

Jimmy stared around frantically, and finally found the big red button at the side of the steering wheel.

"OK," he said firmly. He pressed the flashing red button and Cabbie's engine roared into life.

"A little revving for show," said Cabbie, gunning his engine, then reeling in the magnet as fast as he could, "and here we go! We're off...!"

Jimmy jammed his foot down on the accelerator and they burst out onto the winding track on a ridge high inside the Grand Canyon.

"Don't look down, Jimmy," Cabbie warned.

"Why not?" answered Jimmy, looking down – and immediately regretting it. He saw a sheer drop to the thin silver line of the river about a mile below.

His heart climbed into his throat and he gripped the steering wheel like he was hanging on for his life. Then he focused on the road ahead, steering steadily between the cliff face to their left and the drop to their right, aiming for the dust cloud thrown up by the racers ahead.

"We've got to catch them up," he said through gritted teeth. "But I can't even see them."

"I can help with that," Cabbie said. "Push the windscreen zoom." A little purple button popped up on the windscreen and started to flash. Jimmy pressed it, and a corner of the windscreen magnified the glass so it felt like Jimmy was peering through a pair of binoculars.

In the distance, Horace and Zoom were trying to edge past Monster's huge wheels, but the road wasn't wide enough for them both. As Jimmy watched, Zoom did a daring overtake on the winding lane and edged past Missy and Monster. Jimmy had to admit that Horace and Zoom made a pretty good team.

"Come on, Cabbie, we mustn't lose them!" he said determinedly.

"We're gaining on them," Cabbie replied as they shot past a blur of cliff face and sand. "If we can keep this speed up, we'll catch them in..." He paused for less than a second to calculate. "...just under three minutes and seven seconds."

"Let's go, then!" cried Jimmy. He was still sweating and his heart was beating a million times a second, but that feeling of excitement and concentration was taking over the nerves. He had a job to do, and that was to get Cabbie to the finish line as fast as possible.

"Bend in the road ahead," warned Cabbie.

Jimmy remembered a similar winding cliff-top track in one of the races he'd watched last year. Big Al and Crusher had taken it too fast and crashed. He eased off the pedal slightly and took the corner smoothly, before hitting the accelerator once again.

"Nice driving," said Cabbie. They rounded the

bend and Cabbie speeded up as they hit a straight section of track. They could see the other racers ahead in a distant cloud of dust. Jimmy scanned the buttons in front of him for something that could help.

"Hit the rocket-boosters, Jimmy!" cried Cabbie.

"Maybe we should save them," Jimmy replied. "We might need a boost later on." Then he noticed something on the zoom screen. Far ahead, the other racers were being called into a pit stop by their teams.

Chip and Dug got there first, skidding towards the waiting mechanics, who leaped on the racer and went to work. Kako and Lightning were right behind them. Maximus and Zoom bashed into each other, sparks flying, as they crashed into their spaces. In front of Cabbie, Missy and Monster were slowing down for a stop too.

In the last space there was a little figure with wild white hair waving. It was Grandpa.

"First pit stop coming up," crackled Grandpa's voice over the intercom. "Get ready to pull in, Jimmy."

"This is our chance!" Jimmy gasped. "Cabbie, do we really need to stop?"

"Well..." said Cabbie, doing a quick check of his

functions. "Front offside tyre is a little worn, engine might need a little tune-up, spot of oil ... and I need water. And fuel."

"Grandpa?" said Jimmy into the intercom. "Can Cabbie divert water from his water cannon and take fuel from the rocket-boosters?"

"Erm, I don't know, Jimmy. I've never tried it," Grandpa's voice crackled over the intercom.

"Already done it," said Cabbie.

"Brilliant!" cried Jimmy. "We're going on!"

Grandpa stood open-mouthed as they sailed past him, past all the other racers, and went into the lead. In his mirror, Jimmy could see the small white-haired figure, bouncing up and down and punching the air.

Over the intercom came Grandpa's voice. "Go, Jimmy, go!"

Jimmy cheered – and then panicked. He'd never seen a robot racer miss a pit stop before. What if it was the wrong thing to do?

"How far is it to the next pit stop?" he asked anxiously.

"Forty-two kilometres," said Cabbie.

"Will we make it all right?"

"Make it?" cried Cabbie. "Of course we'll make it! There are bits of me that spent twenty years on the taxi circuit! Those other racers might need their fancy paintwork touched up and their wheels massaged, but with enough water and fuel *we* can keep going for ever!"

Jimmy grinned as Cabbie switched on the zoom screen to show the view behind them. He was sure the other racers would catch up soon, but for the moment, they were actually winning!

CHAPTER ELEVEN
Dirty Tricks

The road started to climb and Cabbie accelerated. They snaked left, then right, then left again, Jimmy growing in confidence all the time. The road began to narrow until the ledge they were driving on was only slightly wider than Cabbie's bonnet. Jimmy glanced over at the sheer drop on their right and his stomach did a couple of nervous somersaults.

"No one can overtake us here!" shouted Cabbie, just as the other robot racers appeared in their mirrors. They were gaining fast.

"Whoa!" yelled Jimmy as they rounded a bend and Cabbie's back end swung out over the edge of the cliff. "Let's keep all four wheels on the road, Cabbie."

As the taxi found its grip again, Jimmy heard a faint cheer from the crowd watching from the canyon's edge. Jimmy surged forwards before guiding Cabbie into another right-hand corner.

"Look out!" cried Jimmy, slamming on the brakes as he saw that the road ahead was completely blocked by a huge rockslide. But the racer was still skidding towards the mountain of rocks and boulders ... Jimmy stiffened, bracing himself for the impact.

"Don't worry, I've got this all under control," said Cabbie calmly, hitting the retro-rockets, which fired instantly, bringing them to a stop just in front of the rockslide. As Jimmy peered through the windscreen he could see Cabbie's front tyres smoking, and a cloud of dust had flown up all around them.

Next to them the cliff dropped down to the river below, a tumbling slope of red rocks and dust.

"I didn't see this from the airship," Jimmy complained.

"It wasn't there before," Cabbie confirmed. "I think this is the first challenge of the race. You know there are always obstacles on each track."

Jimmy glanced nervously at the vertical rock face on his left, at the sheer drop down into the canyon on his right, and at the rock pile ahead. "Can we get over it?" Jimmy thought out loud. "Or through it? Or under it?"

"The others are gaining on us," said Cabbie. "Whatever we do, we need to do it fast!"

"OK," said Jimmy. "How do we get over it?"

"We…" Cabbie paused and thought, his computer whirring. "We fire the pogo-thruster. The button's flashing blue now."

"The pogo-thruster?" repeated Jimmy nervously. "What does it do?"

"Rockets us into the sky," said Cabbie. "We'll land on the other side of the landslide and we'll be away."

"But it's a windy day. What if we don't land on the other side?" asked Jimmy. "What if·it rockets us into the sky and we're blown down into the Canyon?"

"Good point," said Cabbie.

"So can we get round it?" asked Jimmy.

"There's a ledge about thirty centimetres wide at the edge of the landslide," said Cabbie. "We reverse, get up to 150 k.p.h., go up on two wheels and—"

"And crash over the edge," finished Jimmy. "Or crash into the landslide. Have you got any suggestions that don't involve us crashing?"

Cabbie thought for a moment. "No," he said.

"Let's back up and get a proper look at it," said Jimmy.

Cabbie quickly reversed. But as he did so, Lightning appeared from nowhere and zipped round him, heading straight for the landslide. At the last moment, steel ropes and grappling hooks flew from Lightning's front shield, grabbed hold of the rock face and pulled Princess Kako and her robobike up and over the mound of fallen rocks like a giant spider.

"We need to do something. Here comes Monster!" said Jimmy, looking in the rear-view display screen. But it was too late. Missy and her enormous monster-truck racer swerved round them. The truck's front grille dropped down and out came a vast drill bit the size of a robo-rocket, spinning into a blur. Dust and rocks and splinters flew up as the drill burrowed into the ground and Monster disappeared down the tunnel she had dug beneath the landslide.

"Now's our chance," cried Jimmy, stamping on the

accelerator. "Let's follow them!"

Cabbie's engine roared, and they flew backwards.

"Oops," said Cabbie. "Still in reverse!"

Jimmy flicked the gear paddle into first gear, but before he could power forwards, Sammy and his hoverbot Maximus had barged in front of them and skimmed into the darkness of the tunnel.

"Come on!" cried Jimmy as Zoom, then Dug, hurtled past and headed for the opening.

"Fire the jet-thrusters and let's get going!" yelled Cabbie.

Jimmy was reaching for the flashing green button when they heard a screech of tyres at the entrance to the tunnel.

Zoom had stopped and Jimmy could see Horace pressing all sorts of buttons on the roof of the sports car.

"What's he doing?" Jimmy cried. "He's blocking the way!"

"Even Horace Pelly can't be that stupid," said Cabbie. "He won't win sitting there!"

"And neither will we," groaned Jimmy.

But a nasty grin had spread across Horace's face.

"Dig your way out of this one, Chippy," he yelled over the roar of his engine.

Two pipes shot out from beneath Zoom's bumper. One sprayed water all over the racetrack. The other sent clouds of white smoke billowing across it. When it cleared, the water had frozen and turned the track into a dangerous ice rink!

Dug was racing towards the tunnel at top speed and when he hit the ice, he had no hope of controlling the racer. The caterpillar tracks tried desperately to grip the path, but they just spun and spun. Dug's pincer arm flailed and grabbed at the ice, helplessly trying to steady himself as he skidded towards the cliff edge.

Jimmy watched Chip's mouth open in a silent, terrified scream as he plunged backwards and disappeared over the side of the cliff...

CHAPTER TWELVE
Over the Edge

Jimmy sat frozen for a moment – long enough to see Horace and Zoom shooting off through the tunnel. Then he jumped out of Cabbie and ran to the cliff edge, inching forward slowly to peer over the edge.

All Jimmy could think about was what he would see when he looked over the edge: the twisted and gashed metal of the broken robot, and Chip...?

Hardly daring to open his eyes, he looked out over the cliff edge. The floor of the Canyon was about a kilometre below them. Jimmy screwed up his eyes in the blazing heat of the sun, but all he could see was dust and sand and rocks. There was no sign at all of

Dug or Chip at the bottom of the canyon.

"*Help!*" cried a voice. It sounded American ... like Chip.

"*Help! Help! Help!*" replied the echoes, rebounding from the towering Canyon walls.

"Did you hear that?" asked Cabbie.

"I heard it!" said Jimmy. "Chip," he shouted down. "It's Jimmy. Are you all right? Where are you?"

"Down here!" said the American voice.

Jimmy moved along the cliff face, trying to edge closer to where the sound was coming from. When he found the spot he stretched a little further out over the Canyon. Fighting the dizzying view beneath him, he looked straight down – squinting against the glare of the sun as it bounced off the shiny surface of ... Dug!

Jimmy cheered. There, resting about 20 metres directly below them, was the huge yellow racer. Dug appeared to be hanging in mid-air and Chip's head was poking out of the window, looking up at Jimmy and waving.

"Hold on!" Jimmy yelled down. The echo of his voice sent a few small stones from the rockslide showering over the cliff face. They plummeted down, down, down and then bounced!

"It's an invisible force field," said Cabbie to Jimmy. "Dug's scanners are showing a high-voltage plasma net down there."

"Lord Leadpipe must have had them installed for the race because he expected at least one of us to end up being knocked over the edge," Jimmy guessed.

He racked his brains for a way to help them up. None of the safetybots were hovering overhead. There was no sign of anyone at all who could help rescue Dug and Chip. It was up to Jimmy. He ran over to Cabbie and got in.

"What are we doing?" said Cabbie. "Let's fire up the engines and catch those other losers!"

"We're not going anywhere," said Jimmy.

"What?" said Cabbie.

"We've got to help Chip and Dug," said Jimmy. "We're their only hope!" He scanned the rows of buttons on his control panel, looking for something he could use to help Chip – retro-rockets, jet-thrusters, rocket-boosters, Magnetic SuperPull...

"Yes!" cried Jimmy excitedly, remembering the

huge magnet flying out of Cabbie's roof at the start of the race. "Cabbie, I'm firing the Magnetic SuperPull over the cliff edge. OK?"

"I can do better than that," replied Cabbie. "Press the green button. It's flashing now."

"What is it?" asked Jimmy, punching the button.

"The Magnetic Superpull Crane-o-matic," replied Cabbie proudly. And before Jimmy could say ask any more questions, he felt four heavy thuds as stabilizing legs extended from Cabbie's undercarriage.

Jimmy opened his window and stuck his head out to get a better view. A hatch opened on Cabbie's roof and an enormous crane arm rose high into the air, stretching out like a tape measure over the cliff edge. Then he heard a familiar click and a rush of air as the Magnetic SuperPull fired out of the roof and flew down into the Canyon.

"Just like going fishing," Cabbie said, a smug edge to his voice. "Not that I've ever been fishing before."

Jimmy got out of Cabbie and hurried back to the cliff edge. The huge magnet swung on its chain from the crane arm, about two metres short of Chip and his massive racer.

"It's not long enough!" called Chip.

Oh, no, thought Jimmy. *There's no way of getting closer to them.*

Then suddenly he had an idea.

"Chip, you're going to have to reach up as far as you can. If you can get Dug's lifting arm close enough, the magnet will do the rest."

Everything seemed to be happening in slow motion. For a split-second it looked as if they were still too far away. The magnet swayed from side to side as Dug's long arm stretched to breaking point to reach it.

Come on, come on, Jimmy thought.

Then suddenly there was a loud *thunk!* that echoed around the Canyon.

"Yes! Reel them in, Cabbie!" called Jimmy.

Cabbie braced himself on his four stabilizing legs, tightened the chain and began to heave.

Slowly Cabbie pulled Dug up. The digger swayed to and fro in the wind as it was hauled up. Clouds of black smoke poured from Cabbie's exhaust as he strained against Dug's enormous bulk, his engines firing on full throttle to generate enough power for the super-electromagnet.

"Yee-haa!" yelled Chip, punching the air in celebration as they gradually emerged from the Canyon. Still creaking and groaning, Dug rose level with the racetrack, and Cabbie swung the Crane-o-matic's huge arm around and gently lowered Dug to the ground.

"That's some gadget!" called Chip, jumping down from his cab. "Thanks, guys. I thought we was a goner when we went flyin' over the edge." His face suddenly darkened. "I can't wait to get Dug's claws on that Horace fella and his robot."

"No problem," said Cabbie. "Now, does anyone think we should get going?"

"The race!" cried Jimmy and Chip together.

Chip jumped into Dug, and Jimmy jumped into Cabbie and, side by side, they fired up their engines.

"After you!" called Chip. "It's the least I can do!"

Jimmy nodded his thanks, and Cabbie shot through the gap in the landslide with Dug following close behind. They flew out the other side of the tunnel to the deafening roar of hundreds of fans cheering, the noise spurring the two racers on to even greater speeds.

"Hello? Hello?" crackled a familiar voice on Cabbie's intercom.

"Grandpa!" said Jimmy.

"Where are you?" said Grandpa. He sounded worried. "Four of the other competitors have made their second pit stop already."

"We had a bit of a problem," said Jimmy. "All sorted now."

"I don't know what you've been doing to him," said Grandpa, "but it looks like Cabbie's blown seven or eight fuses and your rocket fuel's nearly on zero. That wipes out the rocket-boosters and you're going to need them. Pit stop in two kilometres. You'd better pull in this time."

"Another hold-up?" grumbled Cabbie. "Rock falls, rescue missions, pit stops ... why don't we stop for a cup of tea and a slice of cake as well?"

"Come on, Cabbie," said Jimmy. "Grandpa needs to check you over. We'll never win if you're not in peak condition. There it is!"

Cabbie slowed and pulled into position at the pit stop, just seconds ahead of Chip and Dug.

Grandpa stuck his head in the window, filling the

cab with his huge white hair. "You're doing brilliantly, my boy." He grinned. "I'll get under the bonnet and have a quick tune-up and you can get on your way."

Jimmy sat patiently while Grandpa ran a computer check on Cabbie's functions and made some small adjustments. Grandpa danced around the taxi like a man half his age, inserting a new microchip here and replacing a blown fuse there.

After just a few moments he shouted, "All clear! Off you go, my boy. Sock it to 'em."

"Right," said Jimmy as Cabbie fired up his engines. "Time for some speed, Cabbie. I'm putting my foot down."

"About time!" exclaimed Cabbie, his tyres squealing. "Full speed ahead!"

CHAPTER THIRTEEN
Back in the Race

Jimmy and Cabbie hurtled out of the pit lane in a cloud of dust, as Chip's mechanics climbed all over Dug, tightening bolts and hammering out dents after the bashing he had taken. Monster, Zoom, Maximus and Lightning were nowhere to be seen.

"We've got some catching up to do, Cabbie," said Jimmy.

"Rocket-boosters?" suggested Cabbie.

"Not yet. Not yet. There's a long way to go and we might need them for a fast finish."

They sped on for the next few miles without any incidents, both Cabbie and Jimmy staying silent, focused on the track in front of them. But as they rounded a bend and began to climb a long, steep hill, they got their first glimpse of another competitor.

Crawling up it, just ahead of them, were Missy and Monster.

"Why are they going so slowly?" asked Jimmy.

"Too heavy to get up the hills," said Cabbie, preparing to overtake.

Cabbie darted to the right of Monster.

Monster swerved to the right and blocked him.

Cabbie darted to the left.

Monster blocked him again.

"And too wide and too sneaky for us to get past," muttered Cabbie in frustration.

"What do we do?" asked Jimmy.

"I've got it!" said Cabbie. "I know a way to get past Missy before you can say, 'Cabbie that was amazing, you're a genius.' OK?"

Jimmy nodded.

"Right," said Cabbie. "Drop back. We need" – Cabbie paused to calculate – "fifty-seven metres between us and Monster."

Jimmy eased off the accelerator and soon the gap

between Cabbie and Monster widened.

"Perfect," said Cabbie. "Now maintain that speed and, when I say so, press the flashing orange button on the top right of the control panel."

"OK," said Jimmy, gritting his teeth.

"Ready? Now!" said Cabbie. Jimmy pressed the orange button. With a *whoosh!* and a flash of black, a rocket shot out from under Cabbie's bonnet. It soared high into the air, then arced downwards sharply. As it plummeted back towards earth it unfolded into a steep ramp which hit the ground with a *thud!* just behind Monster.

With a whoop of excitement Jimmy crushed the accelerator pedal to the floor and gripped the steering wheel for dear life. They hit the ramp at top speed and flew high over the monster truck. In a strange, still moment of silence, Jimmy could see nothing through Cabbie's windscreen but blue sky. His stomach seemed to be in his throat. He didn't dare breathe. Then Cabbie began to tip forward … forward … forward … and landed with a skidding thump, kicking up a mountain of dust behind them.

"Amazing!" screamed Jimmy. "Genius!"

"Thank you," said Cabbie calmly. "I've been looking forward to using the VelociRamp."

"Drat!" they heard Missy shout as they roared away over the brow of the hill. "Monster, you great big dingo, why do you have to be such a lardy boot?"

Leaving the red-haired girl and her racer far behind, Cabbie and Jimmy flew over the top of the hill and tore down the other side.

"Now, let's find the others and get past them," Jimmy said. He hit the windscreen zoom-in button. It showed Horace Pelly and Zoom in the lead, Sammy and Maximus just behind them, and Princess Kako on Lightning bringing up the rear of the group.

"I'm at top speed," said Cabbie, soaring round a bend on two wheels. "We'll catch them in the next five minutes."

"Excellent," said Jimmy as Cabbie continued to eat up the miles.

Zoom was now in the lead with Maximus and Lightning right behind him, dodging left and right, looking for space to overtake. The road narrowed and the cliff face crumbled as Maximus slid dangerously close to the edge. All three robot racers were now bumping and jostling each other, swerving wildly and taking risks to get the upper hand.

Maximus made another dart towards the left, but before he could drag himself alongside the sleek black shape of Zoom, there was a deafening noise that made Jimmy's stomach wobble and his ears throb. Suddenly the giant hovercraft seemed to hit an invisible wall. It flew high into the air, spinning back over the roof of Cabbie as if it were a paper bag being tossed around in the wind.

"What the…" Jimmy whispered.

"He's going over the edge too," Cabbie said.

But Cabbie was wrong. Maximus was swept into a vicious-looking clump of cacti. As Jimmy sped past he heard a long, loud *RRRRRRRRIIIIIIIIIIIIPPPPP!* The cacti tore a deep hole into the bottom of the racer's air cushion and the gas inside came whooshing out, making a low hissing noise.

Sammy climbed out awkwardly, trying to avoid the nasty spikes on the nearest cactus. When he saw the tear in the side of his racer, he scowled and stamped his foot. There was no way he could carry on today. Sammy and Maximus were out.

"Wow!" breathed Jimmy, forcing his eyes back onto the road in time to see something glowing above Zoom's rear bumper: a coil of pulsing blue light.

"What's that?" he shouted.

"It looks like Zoom's using some kind of EMP," replied Cabbie. "That's short for Electromagnetic Pulse. A kind of force field. It burns out electrical circuits on anything that comes near it. That's what threw Maximus off the track. The moment anyone tries to overtake Zoom, he'll fry their circuits!"

CHAPTER FOURTEEN
The Finish Line

Cabbie and Lightning raced side by side, both keeping a safe distance from Zoom and his deadly EMP.

"There's no way we can win if we're stuck behind Zoom," said Jimmy impatiently. "We've got to do something."

"The pogo-thruster!" cried Cabbie. "We can be up and over him before you can say—"

"No," said Jimmy. "We'll jump straight off the cliff. I've got another plan. You get as close as you dare. Pull to the right like you're going to overtake. He'll swerve right to block us. So we dart left. The track's wider here. If we can get past Zoom on the inside fast enough, we might get through without getting fried."

"That sounds dangerous," said Cabbie. "I like it!"

As they hurtled towards Zoom, all Jimmy could focus on was the pulsing blue coil above the black racer's rear bumper. It buzzed and growled like the noise made by a hundred microwaves all working at once. He could feel the air crackling with electricity as the EMP reached full charge again.

"Here we go," said Cabbie, his voice shaking with the speed.

"Go, Cabbie, go!" Jimmy cried, squashing the accelerator as hard as he could, and swerving first one way then darting to the other, just as they'd planned. The taxi's engine roared and they began to pull alongside Zoom. "Yes. We're doing it," Jimmy yelled. "We're going to make it!"

The air suddenly fizzed and a wave of hot energy rolled over Cabbie as Horace fired the EMP.

"If I can just—" began Cabbie. "I think—" he went on, "engine what magnet..." He mumbled as he started to lose power, "...fried magnet monster."

"Cabbie?" Jimmy cried in alarm. "What's wrong?"

A large orange triangle started flashing and

blinking on Cabbie's control panel.

"Error. Error. Error…" said Cabbie repeatedly, his voice fading into silence. They were slowing down, dropping back from Zoom, now level with Lightning.

"Ha, ha! You're finished now, Roberts," Jimmy heard Horace shout over the noise of the racers. "Your old rustbucket never stood a chance against Zoom."

But Jimmy didn't care about Horace Pelly at that moment. He was too worried about his friend. "Cabbie?" he said urgently. "Cabbie? Talk to me." He stamped on the accelerator.

Nothing happened. The roar of Cabbie's engines fell to a sickly whirr, and then silence. Lightning was thirty metres ahead of them and Zoom a hundred metres ahead of Lightning. Soon Cabbie would come to a standstill.

Jimmy started frantically pushing buttons but nothing happened. "Don't give up, Cabbie. We're so close to the finish."

Suddenly there was a loud *beep* and every light and button on Cabbie's huge control panel started flashing, randomly at first, and then in sequence.

At the same time, Zoom began to lose speed and

the blue coil of pulsing light dimmed. The grinding noise faded and Jimmy could feel cold, fresh air on his face once again, as Cabbie's cooling systems returned.

The orange triangle on the control panel stopped flashing and the hum of Cabbie's power returned, from a whirr, to a purr, to a growl, to a roar.

"Hah!" shouted Cabbie. "That EMP uses thousands of volts a second. Using it twice in a row has sapped Zoom's power. Let's go!"

"Are you feeling OK?" asked Jimmy.

"Much better," said Cabbie. "There's nothing like a total re-boot and self-repair to set you up for the day." He shot back up to full speed, and within seconds he had drawn level with Zoom.

From the corner of one eye, Jimmy caught a glimpse of Horace shouting and spitting in fury and pounding at Zoom's controls with his fists. "Come on, you hunk of junk," he was shouting. "I won't be beaten by that rubbish excuse for a robot racer."

Cabbie edged ahead, but Zoom was quickly getting back to full power himself. As the road widened and the finish line got nearer, three racers –

Cabbie, Lightning and Zoom – were side by side, neck and neck.

Jimmy glanced across at Princess Kako in her silver motorcycle leathers and helmet, her face hidden behind a smoked black visor. Then he fixed his eyes back on the road, concentrating on every bend, every rock, every millimetre of the racetrack.

Without warning, a thundering blaze of flame exploded from Lightning's exhaust pipe and Princess Kako shot ahead at an incredible speed.

"Time for the rocket-boosters, Jimmy!" said Cabbie. "The red button's flashing."

"Not yet, Cabbie," said Jimmy, his voice calm and steady as Lightning sailed into the distance. "We only have ten seconds of rocket fuel left in the tank because we used some up earlier. We've only got one chance, so we've got to get it right."

He glanced across at Zoom. For a moment, his eyes met Horace's and Jimmy saw the other boy's gritted teeth, his face creased with anger.

Not looking so smug now, is he? Jimmy thought.

"Come on, come on, we need rocket-boosters now!" Cabbie yelled again.

"Not yet, Cabbie," shouted back Jimmy above the roar of the engine. "Not yet."

"But look!" shouted Cabbie. "The finish line! Just over one kilometre."

Ahead, a huge crowd had gathered at the finish line and the black and white chequered flags were flapping in the Nevada wind.

"Finish line in 0.7 kilometres," said Cabbie.

Jimmy rested his finger on the flashing red rocket-booster button.

"Finish line in 0.5 kilometres," warned Cabbie, his voice getting higher and more urgent. Zoom and Cabbie hurtled towards it, getting every last ounce of speed out of their engines.

Jimmy wiped his sweating hand on his jeans, and rested his finger on the flashing button once more.

"Finish line in 0.3 kilometres. At current speed, that's in *ten seconds*," Cabbie cried.

Princess Kako and Lightning were getting further away and nearly across the finish line. *We can't catch Princess Kako*, Jimmy said to himself. *But there's no way I'm letting a spoilt brat like Horace Pelly beat me.*

He locked eyes with Horace as the two racers

touched wheels. Sparks flew off their bodywork and Horace gnashed his teeth in frustration. As the princess crossed the line, punching a fist into the air and saluting the screaming crowd, Jimmy took a deep breath … and pressed the flashing button!

The world blurred for a second as the rocket-boosters fired up. Jimmy was forced back into his seat as Cabbie went from fast to super-fast in a single second.

"Nooooooo!" shrieked Horace as Jimmy and Cabbie hit the line, just 10 centimetres ahead of Zoom.

The crowd roared and the chequered flag waved. As Cabbie fired his retro-rockets to slow them to a stop, Jimmy looked out of the window at thousands of smiling faces looking down on him from the stands.

He stuck his head out of Cabbie's window, raised his hands in the air to salute the fans and shouted, "Yeeeeesss!"

CHAPTER FIFTEEN
The Results

"We did it, Cabbie!" Jimmy whooped in delight.

"Well done, Jimmy," said Cabbie.

"Me?" said Jimmy, grinning broadly. "Well done, Cabbie, I think you mean!"

"We *were* a pretty good team, weren't we?" the taxi replied.

"I didn't think we'd finish the race, let alone come second!" Jimmy laughed. "And we beat Horace Pelly!"

Jimmy watched in disbelief as one by one the other racers crossed the line.

"Come on," said Cabbie, firing up his engines

again, "let's have a look at the results boards." They headed for the main grandstand, where a huge hovering display board was just about to show the final results.

"What are we waiting for?" Jimmy wondered aloud, climbing out of Cabbie. "Everyone knows Princess Kako came first and we came second."

The display boards flashed, numbers whirring, and high above them sailed Lord Leadpipe's airship, his grinning face projected on its side once more.

"Ladies and gentlemen," boomed Lord Leadpipe's voice from the loudspeakers, "the results of this thrilling first leg of the Robot Races Championship are as follows…"

"In first place, with ten points," boomed Lord Leadpipe, "it's … Princess Kako and Lightning." The crowd cheered and the newspaper reporters swarmed around the princess and her robobike, their cameras flashing.

"In second place, with eight points," said Lord Leadpipe, "it's … Jimmy Roberts and Cabbie!"

Jimmy felt his heart swell in his chest until he thought it would explode.

"In third place," said Lord Leadpipe, "it's Horace Pelly and Zoom. But," continued Lord Leadpipe, "Horace Pelly will have two points deducted – repeat two points deducted – following the use of unauthorized gadgetry and suspicious conduct."

"What!" screeched Horace Pelly. "Unauthorized? Suspicious? Is he calling me a cheat? Dad!" he shrieked, stamping his foot. "Dad! Get over here! And bring those NASA idiots with you!"

"So Horace Pelly and Zoom," continued Lord Leadpipe, "are in equal third place on four points with Chip Travers and Dug. Missy McGovern and Monster have two points. Samir Bahur and Maximus did not complete the course and so are yet to score."

Jimmy watched as Horace bellowed at his father and kicked dents in Zoom's doors, but he soon lost sight of them as he and Cabbie were swamped by reporters with cameras and notebooks asking them all kinds of questions.

"How did you feel, knowing you were favourite to come last?"

"How do you feel about coming second?"

"What are your chances in the next race?"

"Who built your racer?"

"What were your tactics?"

Jimmy stood with his mouth opening and closing like a goldfish, and only one thought in his head: find Grandpa.

"I'll answer that question," came Cabbie's voice from behind Jimmy. "At first," Cabbie explained to the journalist, "we played it cool. Keeping our heads down. Not wanting to take the lead, but—"

Jimmy pushed his way through the crowd, leaving Cabbie to enjoy his moment in the spotlight. He was looking for a glimpse of Grandpa's wild white hair. And there it was, bobbing its way towards him. He had his arms outstretched, with a smile so wide it nearly met round the back of his head. Jimmy leaped into Grandpa's arms and they both hugged till they were gasping for breath.

"Well done, my boy," Grandpa finally managed to splutter. "Well done!"

The crowd around them clapped and cheered.

"Thanks for your help out there," said Chip, pushing through the crowd and shaking Jimmy by the hand until his arm ached. "I'd still be there now if you hadn't come along and saved me."

"No problem," said Jimmy.

"Congratulations, Jimmy," said a familiar voice behind him. Jimmy turned slowly to meet the twinkling eyes and rosy red cheeks of one of the richest and most powerful men on the planet – Lord Leadpipe. "You and Cabbie drove a marvellous race. Beautifully done. That's one of the finest performances I think I've seen in all the years we've held the competition. And certainly one of the closest finishes." His smile broadened and he leaned forward to pat Jimmy on the shoulder. "Why don't you introduce me to the rest of your team. Is this your mechanic over here…?" Lord Leadpipe turned to Grandpa. "Good lord," he said. "You're … I mean, it's—"

"Wilfred Roberts," finished Grandpa coldly. "Hello, Ludwick. It's been a long time."

"It's so nice to see you after all these years," Lord Leadpipe said, a smile spreading across his very-famous face. But what are you doing here?"

"Jimmy's my grandson," explained Grandpa, his voice growing colder. "And I built his racer, Cabbie. You see, Ludwick, my robot might not be as flashy and shiny as some of yours, but I've still got a few robo-tricks up my sleeves."

"Well," said Lord Leadpipe, looking flustered, "it's – it's lovely to see you again."

"Is it?" snapped Grandpa. "I wish I could say the same."

"Oh dear," said Lord Leadpipe, his monocle dropping out of his eye and his face turning an even deeper shade of red. "Well," he went on, trying to fix a smile on his face as a swarm of newspaper reporters and photographers surrounded them, "you've got a grandson to be proud of. I noticed him stopping off to help one of the other competitors who had got into a spot of bother, even though he knew it would probably cost him the race. It's not every driver that would do such a thing. Either of you," said Lord Leadpipe turning to Jimmy and Chip, "could have won that race, you know."

Jimmy and Chip went bright red and stared at the ground, each burning with pure pleasure. "And who knows," added Lord Leadpipe, "one of you may well win the next leg of the Robot Races Championship. Talking of which, I have an announcement to make."

Lord Leadpipe waved a hand in the air and Joshua Johnson, the robot co-ordinator with the enormous eyebrows, came running over with a microphone. He still had cotton wool stuffed deep in his ears.

"Ladies and gentlemen," Lord Leadpipe said into the microphone, his voice ringing out around the Grand Canyon. "I am delighted to announce that the next stage of the Robot Races Championship will take place in just one month's time. I can't reveal where just yet – but rest assured it will be another action-packed, adrenaline-fuelled, no-holds-barred fight to the chequered flag! We look forward to seeing you all there! And remember, *keeeeep* racing!"

Jimmy and Grandpa looked at Cabbie, and then at each other, their eyes twinkling with excitement.

"A month?" said Cabbie, revving his engines. "Grandpa, get your spanner, we've got work to do! Today's race might be finished – but the championship's only just begun!"

ROBOT RACES

RESULTS TABLE

RACE 1: CANYON CHAOS

Race Position	Racer	Robot	Points
1	Kako	Lightning	10
2	Jimmy	Cabbie	8
3-	Horace	Zoom	4
3-	Chip	Dug	4
5	Missy	Monster	2
6	Sammy	Maximus	0

Turn over for a sneak peek of the next Robot
Races adventure ... *RAINFOREST RAMPAGE*

RAINFOREST RAMPAGE

"Come on, Cabbie! You can do it!" shouted Jimmy at the top of his voice. Cabbie squealed around a corner, his back end swerving away from the road. He was going so fast he nearly toppled over the side of the narrow track into the deep canyon below. The wheels span as the robot racer tried to speed off, sending a cloud of dust up into the air.

"Well, hot dawg! If that ain't the slyest, smartest bit of driving I seen in years!" said the American commentator on the TV.

Jimmy smiled proudly. "Watch your speed, Cabbie!" he shouted at the old, flickering television. Of course, he had no reason to worry. He knew exactly what would happen next in the race – he had been driving Cabbie at the time.

Jimmy and his best friend Max were sat on the mouldy old sofa in Jimmy's living room, watching a re-run of the first stage of the Robot Races Championship. On the screen the plume of dust and exhaust smoke settled to show Cabbie racing along the sandy track, a heat haze rising in front of him. The camera rose to show the other contestants.

There was Princess Kako in her silver leathers, riding her robobike, Lightning. She looked effortlessly cool as she zipped along the track.

Chip, the American racer, was next in his large yellow digger-like robot called Dug. The size and weight of Dug meant that he didn't look as elegant as Princess Kako, more like a terrifying herd of buffalo stampeding down the track.

In his deadly-looking hoverbot Maximus, Samir – the quiet Egyptian boy – swept by as smoothly as a skater across an ice rink.

Missy, the Australian tomboy, trundled along in her four-wheeled giant racer, Monster.

Finally the camera panned to show the sleek black

racing-car like robot named Zoom, and Jimmy winced as the camera turned to its driver, Horace Pelly. Horace had been annoying enough when Jimmy was at school with him, but now they were racing against each other, he had hit new levels of smugness. Jimmy couldn't believe it when Horace flipped the visor up on his helmet and winked at the camera, his gleaming white teeth reflecting in the sunlight before he accelerated off down the track.

Jimmy rolled his eyes at Horace. *What a show off*, he thought.

On the TV the racers were coming to the final section of the track and Jimmy allowed himself a grin. After all, he knew how the race ended!

"This is shaping up to be one of the most exciting finishes of a Robot Race ever!" bellowed the TV commentator.

"Go, Cabbie, go!" Max whooped in the living room, bouncing up and down on the sofa like a jack-in-a-box.

Jimmy watched as he saw himself and his rickety robot Cabbie closing in on the two state-of-the-art robots, Lightning and Zoom.

Jimmy had been watching the Robot Races for years and he still couldn't believe that now he was actually taking part in them. Even though he knew how it all turned out, he couldn't help feeling nervous as he watched himself speed down the home straight. With the finish line in sight, Princess Kako had opened up a gap between herself and the other two racers, leaving Jimmy and Horace battling it out for second place.

"Fire your rocket-boosters!" Max shouted at the TV, and Jimmy grinned. It was so strange to hear his best friend cheering him on in the same way that they'd always cheered for their favourite robot racers.

On the flickering screen, the other Jimmy held his nerve, waiting until the last moment to use his boosters. With the chequered flag in the air just a few hundred metres away, there was an explosion of fire from Cabbie's thrusters. The rockets propelled him across the line into second place.

"Yes!" yelled Jimmy.

"Awesome!" shrieked Max.

They leaped up in the air and high-fived before doing a little jig together in the middle of the room.

Jimmy immediately felt a bit silly celebrating a finish which had taken place over a week ago, but the re-run was the first chance he'd had to see the race since he'd taken part in it. The TV cut to the commentators in the studio.

"Well, I'll be…! It don't get more exciting than that! Princess Kako rockets into first place, while underdog Jimmy Roberts from" – the presenter paused while he tried to say the name of Jimmy's town – "Smed-ing-ham in the UK takes second. A fine performance, and we're not the only ones who think so!"

The TV cut to a familiar face. Big Al, one of the superstars of Robot Races, stood alongside his robot, Crusher. He was Jimmy and Max's favourite ever contender. Jimmy had posters of Big Al all over his bedroom walls. Max was an even bigger fan. He had once asked his mum if he could get a tattoo of Crusher.

"Big Al, when it was announced that Lord Leadpipe was going to run the Robot Races Championship for children under sixteen years old, did you ever think the talent would be this good?" the interviewer asked.

The large American racer laughed – a big, booming

laugh that shook Jimmy's old TV so hard that the picture frame on top of it slid off and crashed to the floor.

"We all know that Lord Leadpipe likes to shake things up, and he's a smart guy. He knew what he was doing! The racing I've seen from these youngsters has been *crazy*, man! That first race was amazing!" Big Al said, almost spitting out his gum in excitement.

"Who stood out for you?" asked the interviewer.

Big Al turned to look at the camera. "Folks, you only need to remember one name in this competition, and that's Jimmy Roberts."

Jimmy's mouth fell open as he heard his name being mentioned by one of his heroes.

"Jimmy's got it all – speed, style and timing. His racing last week was outstanding!"

Back home, Jimmy could barely breathe with shock. A little bit of dribble left his mouth and plopped onto the carpet.

"The robots this year are great," continued Big Al. "There are some sweet designs out there, but Cabbie's the one to watch. He reminds me of Crusher years ago when I first built him. He doesn't look all that great, but he's got *soul*."

Max jumped up and down on the sofa in excitement, his floppy brown hair swishing in different directions. "Big Al is a fan of *my* best friend. That practically makes him *my* friend! Jimmy, do you think he'd take us for a spin in Crusher?"

But Jimmy was too speechless to reply. He felt like he was in a dream. It was just a few weeks since he had first heard of the special Robot Races Championship for children. And on that very same day he'd learned that his eccentric old grandpa who drove a taxi for a living was actually a robotics genius. Within days Grandpa had knocked together a robot racer made out of his old taxi and some spare parts he had lying around in his shed. The next thing Jimmy knew, he was in the local time trials, and when he sped to victory, he became a contender for the championship. He was whisked off to the Grand Canyon to compete against the best young racers in the world.

Sometimes it felt so awesome that Jimmy thought he might explode.

"Well, I suppose I better get home," Max said. "Mum wants to take me and my nan to the shops."

"Sounds like fun," Jimmy replied, pulling a face as he opened the front door.

"Not really," said Max. "I'll have to spend an hour watching them choose a pair of woolly socks. It's nowhere near as much fun as hanging around with your grandpa."

Jimmy grinned. Max was right: living with Grandpa *was* pretty cool. He watched Max trudge off down the street, then went and peered out of the back window. At the bottom of the garden was a rickety old wooden shed with small dirty windows. It looked like the kind of building that you would use for storing a lawnmower and maybe a couple of spades, but Jimmy knew that behind those doors lay the entrance to his grandpa's secret underground laboratory. It had been built by the most secret department of the Secret Services, and it was where Grandpa had built the world's first-ever robot...

The loud banging continued, followed by some horrible grinding and scraping noises. Grandpa had been down there ever since the previous day, when it had been announced on TV that the next race would be held in South America – a stage that the commentators were already calling "The Rainforest Rampage".

As Jimmy looked at the shed, sparks came flying out of the open window, landing on the uncut grass outside. There was a scary sounding *clang* – then a roar from inside as the whole shed started to shake.

"It's going to take off!" yelped Jimmy. He dashed out of the back door and ran over to the shuddering shack. Putting his hand on the door handle, he braced himself and wrenched the door open.

"All right, Jimmy?" said Grandpa.

"Hi, Grandpa," Jimmy replied, peering down the slope into the underground lab.

Grandpa looked like a crazy scientist with his wild hair and brass goggles. There was soot all over his face and oil spattered on his navy-blue overalls. In his hands he held a large silver rocket which was buzzing dangerously like it contained thousands of angry wasps. Before Jimmy could move, a huge jet of blue flame erupted from it, heading straight for him!

Read _RAINFOREST RAMPAGE_ to find out what happens next!

Look out for more *ROBOT RACES* adventures!

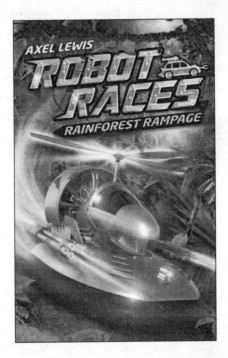

Jimmy and Cabbie are ready for the next race in the championship – a daring dash through the deepest, darkest, jungle. Cabbie's new gadgets might give him an edge, but will he let his fear of snakes hold him back? Jimmy's friend Sammy and his hovercraft robot, Maximus, are right behind them, so every second counts.

With arch-enemy Horace up to his usual tricks, will Jimmy even finish the race?

Jimmy and Cabbie are off again, and this time there are three fiendishly difficult Arctic routes to choose from. Cabbie's been fitted with lots of things to keep them toasty warm, but Jimmy's sneaky arch-enemy Horace and his robot Zoom have got a flamethrower ... and they're not afraid to use it!

Are Jimmy and Cabbie's chances of winning melting fast?

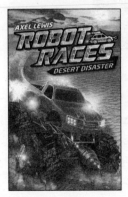

The adventure through the sweltering Sahara desert is a race with no track! Missy and her huge robot, Monster, are used to racing in the Australian outback, but even they are stumped when the robots and their racers have to solve clues to find the right direction. It will take brains as well as gadgets to reach the finish line!

Can Jimmy and Cabbie surf the sand dunes and finish first?

For more exciting books from brilliant
authors, follow the fox!
www.curious-fox.com